To Phyllis —

Blessings & Happy Trails !

Doreen Rawlins

# Glad Reunion

DOREEN RAWLINS

WESTBOW
PRESS®
A DIVISION OF THOMAS NELSON
& ZONDERVAN

Scripture quotations marked NIV are taken from the Holy Bible, New
International Version. NIV. Copyright 1973, 1978, 1984 by International
Bible Society. Used by permission of Zondervan. All rights reserved.

WestBow Press books may be ordered through booksellers or by contacting:

WestBow Press
A Division of Thomas Nelson & Zondervan
1663 Liberty Drive
Bloomington, IN 47403
www.westbowpress.com
1 (866) 928-1240

Because of the dynamic nature of the Internet, any web addresses or
links contained in this book may have changed since publication and
may no longer be valid. The views expressed in this work are solely those
of the author and do not necessarily reflect the views of the publisher,
and the publisher hereby disclaims any responsibility for them.

Any people depicted in stock imagery provided by Thinkstock are models,
and such images are being used for illustrative purposes only.
Certain stock imagery © Thinkstock.

ISBN: 978-1-5127-8963-8 (sc)
ISBN: 978-1-5127-8962-1 (hc)
ISBN: 978-1-5127-8964-5 (e)

Library of Congress Control Number: 2017908500

Print information available on the last page.

WestBow Press rev. date: 06/09/2017

For generations, boys have dominated our family: uncles, cousins, sons, and grandsons. And then one extraordinary day, we were blessed with a girl: our granddaughter, Elle Jane. I had prayed for a girl, just to see what one would look like.

Then, five years after Elle's birth, God blessed us again with Grace Olivia, a second granddaughter. Boys are great. Love all dozen of 'em. But our girls are exceptional. They're beautiful and athletic. They're sweet and funny. They love the Lord and love to bake. Both have a special place in the hearts of their grandparents.

This story is dedicated to Elle and Gracie.

By the way, their lovely images enhance my book covers. Elle Jane is on the cover of *A Little Taste of Heaven*, and Grace is on the cover of *Glad Reunion*.

Love you, girls!

Thatcher Springs Series – by Doreen Rawlins

Book 1 – A Little Taste of Heaven

Book 2 – Glad Reunion

## Part 1

# BETSY MCLEMORE

*See, I am doing a new thing! Now it springs up; do you not perceive it? I am making a way in the desert and streams in the wasteland.*
*—Isaiah 43:19*

# Prologue

## Oregon, 1861

Sloan McLemore lay curled in her bed, shivering. The heavy quilts brought little comfort to her breaking heart. *Thy will be done. Thy will be done. Not my will Lord but yours.* She had cried all night until in the predawn hours a picture came to her mind: Jesus, praying in the Garden. *Thy will be done.* Now she had no tears left, just a cold aching. The black wall she faced became an eerie gray as morning broke, but she lay helpless against the weight of depression.

Sloan could hear quiet movement in the parlor, muted voices. Her breasts ached with nourishment never portioned. *Thy will be done, Lord.* Her eyes blinked wide at the sound—a quiet knock on her bedroom door.

"Sloan?" It was the deep voice of her brother-in-law. "Are you all right, Sloan?"

She bit her lower lip, holding back a sob. "Please, Edward, just go."

Edward lingered. "Are you sure you're—"

"Go *now,* Edward. Please!" Long minutes passed, voices dimming, and then the closing of the front door. She could hear outside as Edward summoned the horses and the carriage creaked to a start. And then all was quiet. Too quiet. *This is how it will be. Forever.*

It seemed like hours passed—or maybe only minutes. Sloan didn't know, nor did she care. She just lay there staring at the wall, trembling. *Thy will be done, Lord.*

A faint sound in the distance barely caught her attention. She heard it again—a soft mewing. Had one of the kittens crept inside? The mewing grew more audible.

Instinctively, Sloan threw back the quilts, slipped from her bed, and raced for the door, her heart beating faster with each step. It was perfectly clear now; the sounds were that of a baby waking. At the sight, Sloan dropped to her knees, no longer able to hold back tears. She scooped up the tiny bundle, holding her tightly and rocking her on the parlor floor. "Oh dear God! My baby girl!"

Through her tears, she saw a note attached to the baby's basket.

> I prayed all night, dearest Sloan, that God's will be done. I believe it is so.
>
> I love you, dear sister.
>
> Alecia

And so it was. Elizabeth "Betsy" McLemore would be raised by her mother out west. Her twin sister, by Aunt Alecia and Uncle Edward, in New York, thousands of miles away on the east coast.

# Chapter 1

"When do ya think we should tell 'em?" Joe asked quietly.

Josh didn't answer right away, thinking about it. "Prob'ly sooner, the better." They had stretched out on their bunks, lying there in the dark, both restless with a mixture of excitement and dread. "I just hope they don't cry."

"You can count on it, Josh. I don't like it either, but we gotta bite the bullet and tell 'em."

The next morning, Kate filled plates with fried potatoes, eggs, and thick slabs of bacon, carefully handing one plate at a time to Ruthie for delivery to the table. Little Annie toddled along behind with a basket of biscuits. The morning sky was pink, the promise of a sunny day. Kate was perspiring from the hot stove but humming with contentment at the sounds of her family scraping chairs on wood floors and gathering at the breakfast table. Max bounced little Max on his knee as Jake lured the family dog out the back door with a piece of bacon. Josh and Joe, Max's twin brothers, came in as the dog went out and pulled up to their places at the table. "Good mornin'," they said in unison as they looked at each other.

"Good mornin'," Max replied as Annie handed each twin a biscuit from her basket. "Annie darlin', let each one get his own biscuit," Max advised. He had the feeling Josh and Joe were up to something. They had always been schemers, and Max could read them like a book. At least, most of the time. "You two sleep good?"

"Yes!" they answered a little too quickly.

Josh continued. "I slept real good. How 'bout you, Joe?"

"Oh yeah, me too. I slept better than usual. Real good."

Max studied the two. They weren't boys anymore. Having lost their mama when they were five and then their pa a couple of years later, Max had mostly raised his younger brothers. They had grown up to be fine young men, twenty years old now. "Well, it's good you're well rested. We got a mile of fence to mend today."

Soon as Kate joined them, Max offered thanks to the Lord, and everyone dug in. When he glanced up, Josh and Joe were not eating much but were shoving their food around on their plates. "You boys feel all right? You're usually goin' for seconds by now."

Joe set his fork down and said, "We're goin' to Oregon, Max. Me and Josh." His face was flushed as he cast a glance at Kate.

"Joe! What'd ya do that for?" Josh looked at Joe like he was going to throttle him. "I thought we agreed to wait!"

Kate sat staring at her boys. She had been mother to them since they were nine. They were a family. Of course, Josh and Joey were mostly grown now, but going to Oregon? Did they mean they were moving out?

Just then, Annie knocked over her cup, spilling milk into her lap and onto the floor. She started to cry, and Jake commenced to get after her. Then baby Max let out a howl just as the dog broke in the back door, tracking through the spilled milk. The dog couldn't resist the temptation to chomp the bacon right out of Ruthie's chubby hand just as Max yelled, "Git!" Ruthie started crying over the dog stealing her bacon. Kate sat there, stunned. Finally, through the chaos, Max suggested that the adults should have this conversation after dinner, when the little ones were tucked into bed.

Eventually after Kate and Millie shed some tears, as predicted, everyone settled in to the idea that Josh and Joe would set out for Oregon around June 1. Max would miss them terribly, but he was overjoyed at the same time. After all, it had been a dream passed on to them by their pa many years ago. It was time for them to carve out a life of their own, find their way. Max was confident in his young brothers. They were made of tough stuff. They weren't afraid of hard work, and their faith in the Lord ran deep. "Twinners will be fine," he assured Millie, "just fine." Kate was thankful that the boys had each other, but already she felt a big hole in her heart. She loved them so much.

Spring flew by as Josh and Joe worked on their wagon and packed up their worldly goods. They were determined to keep up with their normal chores, making sure the fences were mended and plenty of wood was stacked in the woodshed. They couldn't wait to go but at the same time hated the going.

Millie, the winsome innkeeper of Inn at Thatcher Springs, organized an elaborate going-away party. Everyone loved Millie's parties! Tantalizing aromas filled the place, drifting outside where tables were set up for dinner on the grounds, since spring weather had turned perfect at just the right time. "One not-so-good thing about all this," Joe murmured to Josh, "is we're probably never gonna eat this good again."

"More truth than poetry, Joe. More truth than poetry."

The boys planned to leave at daybreak, so after stuffing themselves with a selection of pies and Millie's chocolate cake, Silas gathered everyone to pray over Josh and Joe. He asked for God's blessing, for safety and protection, and that something good would happen for them in Oregon. That was when the sniffling began, the part the boys were hoping to avoid. Everyone hugged both boys, wishing them Godspeed. By the time they got to Kate and Millie, Grace and Simone were sniffling too. All the women, in fact, were crying and blowing their noses into lacey, white hankies. The whole crowd grew somber, and Josh and Joe were trying to figure the best way to make their departure.

A voice rose above the hum. Samuel was laughing. "What's everybody so sad for? Thees is happy time!" His smile was bright in the sunset hour. "These boys go on adventure! When they git beeg ranch in Or-ee-gone, we go there for visit them!"

Everyone laughed then, tempering the moment. Samuel's good perspective helped the whole family overcome the sadness they felt at the boys leaving Thatcher Springs. Besides, Samuel had planted a seed in Millie's mind, causing her to feel better about the whole thing.

# Chapter 2

Baker City, September 1876

"I shor am lookin' forward to a good meal and a hot bath!" exclaimed Joshua. They had made the journey without a hitch, camping along the way—first at the place they had broken down so long ago. Eleven years to be exact. The memory of it brought gales of laughter, especially the part about Kate flailing through the air and landing right into Max's arms.

"You reckon God might do that again? Double?" Joe laughed at the thought.

"Prob'ly the only way either one of us will get a girl," said Josh. They joked about it, but both boys admitted they wouldn't mind finding a good wife someday—as long as she took after Kate and cooked like Millie. They also admitted to being homesick, even though the excitement of Oregon grew each day. Most the time, they loved the adventure of it as Samuel had predicted. Except for a bit of a scare crossing the Snake River and an occasional summer storm, the trip went reasonably well. Since inheriting money from Cody, who generously had divvied up the huge amount of gold left him by his father, Josh and Joe made an agreement to give a portion back to the Lord. They had plenty to buy land and cattle in Oregon, so it was only right to share the blessing. At every town or community that had a church, they would leave an envelope with twenty-five dollars.

At last they had made it to Baker City, a town larger than those they had traveled through. A town with more than one church. "Let's find a good dinner house, then a place to spend a night or two. A good bed be real nice, Joey."

"Count me in. That'll give us a chance tomorrow to figure which church to help out."

They made a deal at the livery to leave their animals and store the wagon behind the livery building, where it would be safe for the night. Walking down the dirt street through town, Joshua spotted a small café with a sign that said, "Home Cookin'." "There's a place that looks good, Joe. C'mon. Let's have us some o' that home cookin'."

"Would you gentlemen like coffee?" the waitress asked, mostly out of habit, not really seeing either of them. She seemed preoccupied.

Joe replied first. "Sounds good to me! Black, please." He continued looking up at her as she poured the coffee. Strands of blonde hair escaped her braid, and despite dark circles under her blue eyes, she was pretty. *Real pretty.* She looked at him briefly, then at Josh.

"And for you?" She looked at Josh, then again at Joe, and then at Josh. She set the coffeepot on the table, folding her arms. "Well, I'll be. Twins! I have never in my life seen identical twins!" She smiled a bright smile, exposing a dimple in her right cheek and beautiful, perfect, white teeth. She was studying the boys intently when from the kitchen came a booming voice.

"Betsy! Quit yer jawin' and git in here, pronto!" Betsy whirled around and dashed to the kitchen, evident she was being reprimanded by the cook. On her retreat, Josh and Joe noticed her faded cotton dress and what appeared to be worn work boots beneath it. They watched her bustle around with a tray, delivering orders to tables in the back.

When she returned to take their order, Josh asked what she recommended. She leaned in and whispered, "The place across the street." Laughing at her own joke, she went on. "Well, seriously, the special is stew, but I would order a cold sandwich if I were you. The roast beef is decent, and Mama makes the bread for this place. I brought in a basket fresh this mornin'." She smiled that smile again, holding the attention of her twin diners.

During a dinner of beef sandwiches, coffee, and pie—also baked by Betsy's mama—the boys learned what they could about the area, including where they might get a room and a bath. They found out that after Betsy finished work at the café, she went to a second job at the boardinghouse across the way, helping her mother do the laundry, clean the kitchen, and set up for breakfast.

"No wonder the poor little thing looks so worn out." Joe looked worn out himself, for feeling sorry for Betsy—Betsy McLemore to be exact. She had introduced herself before Josh and Joe finished their meal and paid the bill. Joe couldn't get her off his mind. It just wasn't right the way she had to work such long hours. The way she had to put up with that disrespectful, grumpy cook! The way she smiled, despite it. There was something about Betsy McLemore. Something Joe couldn't quit thinking about. "That was pretty good, Josh. Maybe we should come back for breakfast in the mornin'."

"Sure, Joe. Sure thing." Josh chuckled and gave Joe a knowing look. His brother was quite taken with Miss Betsy McLemore. "Better stick with toast and coffee though."

After a couple of days in Baker City, Josh and Joe knew the town like the back of their hands. Even though they were tempted to try other dining establishments, they took their meals at "Betsy's Place" as they'd come to call it. After all, it wasn't that bad. At least the coffee was good and certainly the pie, baked fresh daily by Betsy's mother. And of course, Betsy herself made everything better, especially to Joe. The three of them chatted comfortably when things were slow, the boys learning more about Baker City. They also learned a little more about Betsy.

It was just her and her mother. Her pa had died before she was born, but she hadn't explained the circumstances of his death and Josh and Joe didn't ask. Evidently, they had owned a ranch outside of town, the place where Betsy was born. Her mama had tried her best to keep up with it but after four years of backbreaking work, with her baby girl in tow, she decided to sell out.

Betsy gazed out the window, recollecting. "I remember Mama painting, 'For Sale' on a board and nailing it to the fence." A kind of melancholy settled over her features. Joe wanted to hug her.

The moment was shattered when from the kitchen came a shout. "Betsy! Get in here. Now!"

"I'm coming." She jumped to attention and hurried to the kitchen.

Josh and Joe had learned that Betsy and her mother attended the Baptist church. Josh thought they should be moving on, but Joe convinced him another couple of days wouldn't hurt a thing, especially since they had been invited to the Baptists' First Sunday potluck. "Guess it wouldn't do any harm," Josh decided. "And ya'll probably agree, for Betsy's sake—her hospitality and all—we should give the money to the Baptists."

"I been thinkin' on that Josh. I been thinkin' maybe ta just give it to Betsy. The envelope. It's pretty evident she and her ma can use it." Joe looked down at the dirt he was shoving around with the toe of his boot. "In fact, if ya agree, maybe make it a little more? Only if ya agree, Josh."

"Well, sure, Joey. I'm in agreement with ya." He chuckled. "Kinda sweet on her huh, brother?" It was a statement more than a question.

Joe's neck turned pink, but he acted like he hadn't heard that part. "We'll need to go to the bank then on Monday mornin', before we leave town." They shook hands on it, as they did with every decision about the money.

The church potluck proved reminiscent of dinners at home, back in Thatcher Springs. Weathered tables spread with faded cotton cloths, the backdrop for huge platters of fried chicken, baked ham, yams, beans, watermelon, cornbread, and yeast rolls. One long table was dedicated to pies—all manner of pies featuring Sloan

McLemore's celebrated wild berry. Betsy dished up big slices for Josh and Joe while the boys ate their meal, knowing it would be first to go. Mother and daughter had spread a blanket in the shade and the four spent a good hour enjoying the meal and even more so the conversation. Joe couldn't keep his eyes off Betsy—the easy way she laughed, her cheeks pink with the warm fall day.

"Would you fellas like to ride out to the ranch this afternoon? Bein' our one day off, me and Betsy most always ride out, visit with Uncle Charlie, take him some leftovers and a piece of pie."

"The ranch?" It was Joe. He looked at Betsy, puzzled.

Betsy laughed. "Guess I never did finish the story. It's a bit long."

The McLemore ranch had been up for sale over a year, with little interest. A few folks contemplated it, but being fourteen miles from town was a drawback. And then the pasture ground was hilly and had to be flood irrigated. As time went by, the place became rundown and overgrown. Sloan was forced to take her daughter and move to town, get a job, and try to keep the bank happy with a payment now and then. She had sold off their cows over time, but if the Lord hadn't intervened by sending Charlie, the ranch she had shared with Jonathon, all their hopes and dreams would be lost forever. She could not let that happen. In honor of her late husband, she was determined to see their place up and running, a thriving cattle ranch once more.

Uncle Charlie, as Betsy had called him from the beginning, was an old-time saddlemaker, a true craftsman. He showed up one day out of the blue looking for a place to settle, a place away from town where he could set up his leather shop. Sloan had worked out a lease deal with him where he would make a payment with each saddle order and contribute to the upkeep of the place. It was in such disarray by then, Sloan didn't expect the old fella could make a dent, but just having someone live in the house would keep the varmints out. Both kinds. The real blessing though was the friendship that grew among Sloan, Betsy, and Uncle Charlie. They looked out for each other and developed a love for one another like family. Sloan thanked God every day that Betsy had a grandfatherly figure in her life. After all, she had never known her father and had no other family. None that she knew of.

An afternoon breeze came up to cool the hot day, making it a pleasant ride out to the ranch. The four cantered easily on the wide dirt road leading east from town. Betsy's horse was getting up there in years, but she loved the old boy—had grown up on him. She leaned forward, whispering something for Patches' ears only. Then she looked over at Joe with such a sweet, innocent look. "It's about a mile to the turn off Joe. Race?" Before Joe could grasp her meaning, she left him in a cloud of dust, riding Patches like the wind.

Sloan laughed at her daughter, hollering at the same time. "Betsy!" She laughed even more as she attempted an apology. "I'm tryin' my best to make a lady outa her, but she's such a tomboy!"

Josh and Joe were quietly amazed as they entered the ranch property. True, it was neglected, overgrown, the fence in disrepair, although signs of some reinforcement in part, some cleanup in spots, and tools spread about with hope for another day. The property itself held promise.

As they walked their horses up a gentle slope, the house came into view. It was a log house with solidness about it, despite hanging shutters and broken steps to the porch. Even though the grass was brown, the porch overlooked rolling pastureland, a peaceful setting.

Josh spoke up. "I can picture your cow herd out here, ma'am, grazing in a lush green pasture." Sloan only nodded, smiling in agreement. She could picture it too. The property beyond the house continued to slope upward until it met thick timbers that bordered nearly all the meadows. The barn and hay storage were both the worst for wear, leaning with age, shingles missing from the roof. "This place has potential, that's for sure," Josh murmured to Joe.

Laughter came from behind them as the ladies greeted Uncle Charlie on the porch. "Well, if I ain't one ol' blessed cowboy! The two purtiest gals in Baker come callin' on ol' Charlie! Looks like there might even be a piece o' pie, under that there checkie cloth!" He laughed a deep chuckle, his two hound dogs howling in agreement.

Betsy made the introductions, Josh and Joe receiving a hardy handshake and sound slaps on the back. Charlie was intrigued about them being twins as much as Betsy. He led the way inside to the "parlor," he joked, which turned out a pleasant surprise: clean and cozy with the smell of leather and coffee. Half the room was Charlie's saddle shop, featuring a saddle in the making. Josh and Joe were fascinated, asking the old man a pile of questions. Uncle Charlie was a very interesting character, probably near seventy years old but thick in the chest, strong hands. His face was as tanned and leathery as the saddle he was making. He had a big smile and even bigger heart, according to Sloan and Betsy. The boys were both feeling there was something familiar about him. The pale green of his eyes, his mannerisms. Neither could quite figure it out.

Sloan served mugs of hot coffee as everyone pulled up to the table and shared the two large slices of Charlie's pie at his insistence. "A little less—shared with friends—is better than the whole pie by myself!"

Betsy gave the boys a tour, riding their horses beyond the meadow, while Sloan discussed business with Charlie. By the time they needed to leave, Josh and Joe felt a real attachment to Charlie. "We sure would be happy to do some fence mendin' for ya, Charlie," offered Josh.

Joe chimed in, "Fence fixin' is our specialty. That and wood cuttin'. And we're not in any hurry to move on," Joe added, thinking of Betsy.

"I s'pose we could work out some kinda trade. Maybe throw a saddle into the deal." Charlie chuckled.

The boys looked at each other, eyes wide. Joe spoke up. "Ya reckon ya got enough fence mendin' to truly pay for a saddle?"

"Son, there's enough broke-down fence on this place to pay for—" He paused, scratching his whiskery chin. "I'd say maybe even two saddles."

11

As they waved good-bye and started down the road, Charlie shouted, "You fellas come on out next week then! And if ya hear anybody in town needin' a saddle, you send 'em out to see ol' Charlie Alexander!"

They were on the road less than fifteen minutes when Josh suddenly pulled his horse to a stop, stirring up a swirl of dust. The others stopped abruptly, Sloan worried he had spotted a cougar. "Did he say 'Charlie Alexander'?"

"Why yes, Josh, that's Uncle Charlie's name. Charlie Alexander."

The boys looked at each other and declared in unison. "Kate's uncle!" There was no doubt it was Clayton's Alexander's brother. Joe took off his hat and slapped it against his leg. "Well, bless Pat! Will wonders never cease."

That night the boys were too excited to sleep, even after the long day. By lamplight they composed a letter to the folks back home, letting them know they were safe in Baker City and especially the part about Uncle Charlie! "We knew there was somethin about him," Joe wrote. "Now our plans are to bunk at the McLemore place and help out with fencing and such, at least for a few weeks." He didn't mention Betsy, even though he wanted to.

It was a good thing Josh and Joe posted their letter first thing Monday morning, because later in the day everything would change.

## Chapter 3

The morning was bright and clear as Josh and Joe finished up breakfast at Betsy's place, all packed up and ready to head out to Uncle Charlie's. Joe had mixed emotions about leaving Betsy, but knowing she would be coming to the ranch next Sunday was better than leaving the region altogether. He would cross that bridge when the time came. Josh read him like a book. "Why don't you sit here and have another cup of coffee, Joe? I'll mosey down to the bank and come back for ya."

Joe knew Josh was looking out for his best interests. "If you're sure ya don't mind, Josh. I *could* use another cup. Just take yer time, brother."

The place was dead quiet that morning, so Betsy pulled up Josh's vacated chair, taking her chances with the boss. "Sunday," she began, "Mama and I could come on out first thing and do church at the ranch. We do that sometimes. Charlie loves it when we do." She smiled that beautiful smile, looking right into Joe's brown eyes.

"Seems like a long time till Sunday," Joe said. He reached across the table for her hand. She blushed, looking down at the empty cup left behind by Josh, but didn't hesitate to take Joe's hand. "I'll miss comin' here each day. Mostly I'll miss you, Betsy McLemore."

Her blue eyes sparkled. "I'll miss you too, Joseph Reed." Their eyes held a little longer.

13

Without warning, gunshots rang out! Joe instinctively ran for the door, Betsy right behind him. Just then, four gunmen raced their horses wildly past them, clearly making a getaway. Townspeople were shouting with panic stricken voices, "The bank! Them varmints held up the bank!"

Joe sprinted down the boardwalk, dread gripping him like a vice. "Josh!" he shouted. He could feel it in his own body. Josh was hurt. His fears were confirmed when he burst through the doors and saw his brother lying there, motionless. The scene was surreal. A woman had also been shot in the shoulder, her baby wailing as another woman attempted to calm him. Chaos surrounded Josh, folks shouting, women crying as they tried to tend to him. Joe knelt next to him, felt for a pulse. It was weak, but Josh was alive. "Someone, get a doctor!" *Lord, please let him live.* At the same time that Joe was praying on Joshua's behalf, he was forming a plan of retaliation. *Those lowdown cowards shot an unarmed man in the back.* "Come on, Josh. You're gonna be okay. Come on now, brother." Tears blurred his eyes as he looked up to see Betsy comin' through the door with the doctor.

Quickly Dr. Cartwright got to work, shouting orders. Sloan rushed in then, hauling a bundle of fresh cloths and a bucket of clean water. It was evident she had assisted the doc before. After checking Josh's vital signs, the doctor ripped open his bloodstained shirt and began to clean the wound. Joe was glad he was already on his knees as his own blood rushed from his head at the sight. Dr. Cartwright instructed Sloan to retrieve several medicine bottles and doctoring tools from his black bag. She knew just what to do.

The bank was cleared out except for a deputy, the bank president, and one other employee. Doc had ordered the wounded Mrs. Smith and her baby be transported to his office, where Mrs. Cartwright would tend to them until the doctor finished up with Josh, the "most seriously injured."

The doctor determined since the bullet was lodged very close to his spine, they would not attempt to move Josh, but Dr. Cartwright would perform surgery right there on the marble floor of the bank. Joe was grateful that his brother was unconscious.

It felt like a bad dream as Joe watched helplessly. Betsy had been helping her mother, but now she knelt quietly next to Joe and simply held his hand. "Everything will be all right," he said, mostly to himself. "Josh will get through this." *Please God, bring him through this.*

Josh was moved to Doc's hospital room, behind his office. It was a small room with only one bed, but Joe hauled his bedroll in there and slept on the floor next to him. Sometime in the night during the second day, he heard Josh moaning. He was waking up. Joe scrambled to get the lamp lit, speaking comforting words as he stumbled in the dark. "It's okay, Josh. You're gonna be fine. I'm right here, brother."

"What happened? Where am I? Ohhhh, man. It hurts, Joe."

Dr. Cartwright had left a small bottle of pain medication with instructions, which Joe didn't hesitate to administer. He couldn't handle the thought of Josh hurting. Between the time the medication took hold and Josh drifted off, back into a deep slumber, Joe described what had happened as best he could. Over the next few days, more of the pieces came together for Josh.

Sloan and Betsy came daily with warm broth, herb tea, and sometimes pudding. The color began to come back to Josh's face after his losing so much blood. "Won't be long!" Betsy exclaimed with a smile. "You'll be eatin' a big piece of Mama's berry pie!"

Joe noticed that when the doctor checked him over one afternoon, he lifted the sheets off Josh's feet and pulled on his toes, pressed here and there, looking intently for a reaction. An uneasy knot twisted in Joe's belly. "So, Dr. Cartwright, when can we get him up? He's doin' real good, don't ya think?"

Dr. Cartwright avoided the question and simply agreed. "He's recovering nicely." That night the boys got to talking about when they were kids. Like the time they hauled a "half-dead Indian" home, the ornery things they did to get rid of Kate's sisters, and a dozen other crazy memories. They laughed so hard it hurt. Josh especially.

When Josh went quiet, Joe looked up at him intently. "I can't feel my feet, Joe. Can't feel my legs. I'm scared. What if I don't ever walk again?"

"You better walk again, brother. I just whittled you a crutch." Joe tried to sound easy, confident. Josh's comment, however, had only deepened his resolve to go after the no-account that pulled the trigger. He was more determined than ever to even the score.

The boys weren't exactly sure where they were going when Doc said Josh could go "home," since the McLemore Ranch was out of the question. Dr. Cartwright said he would need to stop by every day for a while, to check on his patient. Josh still had no feeling in his legs.

They should have known Sloan and Betsy would have it all figured out. A private room was ready and waiting for Josh, just off the boardinghouse kitchen, where Sloan worked. The room had been added years ago, when the owner developed an illness, for the convenience of his wife, Mrs. Bush, to care for him and still run the place. After Mr. Bush passed away, it became a storage room for everything like old furniture, old tack, the kitchen's original cook stove, and hordes of jumbled odds and ends. The girls recruited some help to haul it away, donating anything useful to the Baptist church. Sloan and Betsy scrubbed the room clean and washed the windows facing the backyard. Removing the dark blankets that covered them made a world of difference. They arranged a comfy bed so Josh would be able to look out the windows and into the kitchen when the door was open. They added a side table and a rocking chair that Mrs. Bush had let them take from the parlor.

A week under Sloan's care, Josh began to feel a bit like his old self, if he could only get up on his own, get his legs back. Joe decided he would spend two days at the ranch, starting the work they had agreed on before the bank robbery. It was only right. He knew his brother was in good hands, although it felt strange, the thought of

16

going anywhere without him. First though, Joe had some business to take care of.

The sheriff's office was at the other end of town. It was the first time he'd passed by Betsy's place without stopping. After slinging the reins around a hitching post out front, Joe walked up the plank steps with intention. "Mornin', Sheriff. Any progress in huntin' down those polecat bank robbers?"

"Sit down, son. How's your brother doin'?" Sheriff Stevens didn't seem to be in any hurry. He poured two tin cups of coffee.

"He's paralyzed. Can't walk. That's how he's doin'!" Joe didn't mean to sound so irritated. "Do ya have any leads, Sheriff? Did your posse find tracks?"

The sheriff leaned back in his chair and put his feet on the desk. "We think they might've headed to Canyon City. We've notified the sheriff over there and a few others as well. Course there's a million places the four of 'em could be hidin' out. It's rugged country between here and there."

Joe was frustrated but didn't know what else to do. "Would it help to put up a reward?"

"The thing is, son, we don't have a good description. We know there's four of 'em, but they wore bandanas over their faces. Only got two things ta go on. According a witness, the leader has a scar on his forehead that goes cross his left eyebrow. That's what Mrs. Smith, the other shootin' victim, described. That, plus they all stunk to high heaven. Only other thing, ol' Chet saw 'em ride out. Noticed one of the saddles had a Diamondback skin cross the cantle."

"Thanks, Sheriff. I'll be back in a couple days to check with ya. If anything comes up, could ya let Betsy know? Down at the café?"

When Joe stepped out on the porch, there sat Betsy on Patches, packed like they were going somewhere. She broke into a huge smile at the sight of Joe. "Well, ya'll ready?"

They rode side by side quietly a while, and then finally Betsy explained. "It took some convincin', but I got a couple days off

17

from work. Mama thinks Mrs. Bush could use more help at the boardinghouse, so even if he gives me the boot, won't be any loss."

The ride out to McLemore Ranch passed quickly with Betsy by his side. Somehow, the pretty little thing gave him courage. Joe relaxed and could release some of his pent-up feelings about Josh, including the fear his brother would never walk again. "We had planned to stop at the bank earlier, together. He did it for me."

Betsy was puzzled by his comment. "What d'ya mean he went to the bank for ya?"

"Well," Joe began, looking straight ahead, "he knew I, uh … Well, he knew I wanted a little time with you, Betsy. Alone."

Betsy blushed but turned toward him. "I'm so sorry, Joe. It must feel like you took the bullet yourself. Bein' twins and all."

Joe felt better sharing his feelings with Betsy. He left out the part, however, about the revenge he held for the lowlife that shot his brother. He wasn't proud of that fact, but he couldn't let it go either. He would hunt the robbers down and get even. "For Josh," he told himself.

"I always dreamed of havin' a sister myself," Betsy confessed. "Don't get the wrong idea. I have a good life. Mama is a wonderful mother. My best friend." She leaned forward, stroking Patches' mane. "It just gets lonely sometimes."

# Chapter 4

Sloan came in from the backyard, closing the screen quietly but leaving the door open hoping for a breeze to cool the house. She peeked in on Josh and found him sleeping soundly. Quietly she slipped into the kitchen to begin dinner preparations.

In the last few days, she had observed the quiet strength Josh exhibited, his good nature, never complaining. She admired the way the two brothers were so caring of each other. They were obviously made of tough stuff and for being so young displayed deep faith in God. She had witnessed them praying together. Twins. Her heart fluttered. After seventeen years, the pain reared up fresh. Would the guilt ever lift? Sweet Betsy would never know she had a twin sister. It was best that way. Still, many times during earlier years, Sloan had watched her little girl playing tea party with an imaginary friend, talking to her rag doll like they were sisters. Betsy seemed so lonely at times. No one knew about Sloan giving birth to twins, except for her sister Alecia, her brother-in-law, Edward, and the midwife who helped deliver them. Hilly had traveled back east to be nanny to Britta. Britta Lundgren, Betsy's twin sister. Her despairing never ended for the loss of her other daughter. It ensued as deeply as her grieving for Jonathon. The correspondence between Sloan and Alecia was purposely kept to a minimum. Betsy only knew that she had an aunt and uncle and a cousin near her age and that they lived in New York in a big house with servants.

The task at hand, supper for a dozen boardinghouse guests, suddenly shook her from her reverie. Endless work wore her out at times but kept her sane. She mustn't dwell on the dreadful thing she had done all those years past. With intensity, she started peeling potatoes and tossing them in a pot of water.

Dr. Cartwright called in the evening, giving extra time to assist Josh with a sponge bath since Joe was gone for a couple of days. Joe would spend two days on and two days off at the ranch and care for Josh in between. The doc gave his patient a nearly clean bill of health. The wound had healed nicely, though swollen a bit. Of course, there was still no feeling in his legs. Doc tried to be optimistic and so did Josh, but both had grave concerns that he would never walk again.

By the time Sloan had the buffet set with a plentiful meal for the guests, Josh was awake and starving. It had become routine for her to deliver a tray to his room so they could eat together while the guests ate their meal in the dining room. Sloan loved hearing stories from the boys growing up in Thatcher Springs. It was apparent how much he missed and loved his family there. She hoped she could bring him a touch of comfort, be a motherly figure to him in what must be a very lonely and fearful time. Their conversation sometimes turned to talks of God. Sloan began the custom of reading a chapter or two from the Bible after dinner.

They were chatting comfortably one evening when Josh brought up the subject of Joe and Betsy. "I think Joe is smitten with your daughter, ma'am. I know him pretty well, after all."

Sloan laughed. "And I know my daughter. She's head over heels for Joe! I've prayed for a long time that Betsy would meet a wonderful man, one like her father. My Jonathon was the kindest, most caring—" She stopped midsentence, swallowing hard. "Betsy never knew him."

"I surely am sorry, Miss Sloan. He must've been very young."

"Yes." She hesitated for a moment. "He was twenty-five." Bitterness hardened her features. "Murdered by cattle thieves." Sloan stood and quickly gathered their plates, hastily taking them to the kitchen.

On another evening, Josh was complimenting Sloan on her good cooking. "Right up there with Millie Thatcher." He went on to share some about Millie's life, how her daughter Grace had been taken by the Indians, Millie not knowing if she was dead or alive. "Then a miracle happened." He went on to tell Sloan about the amazing way God, after nearly twenty years, had brought Millie's daughter home. "Millie is a woman of great faith. She never gave up, all those years not seeing her girl."

Sloan could relate, but she said nothing. It had been seventeen years since she had seen her girl as well. *Lord, I don't know how much longer I can live this lie.*

———

Meanwhile out at McLemore Ranch, Joe and Betsy were making good headway. It was a complete surprise that Betsy's intention was to roll up her sleeves and build fence right along with Joe. Working together surely made it a pleasure, especially when she looked at him and smiled. A time or two they brushed against each other and one time Joe backed right over her as she knelt to stretch a low wire. Joe's heart did a flip-flop each time. They had blushed and apologized simultaneously, then laughed. "You're the purtiest fence mender I've ever had the pleasure to work with, Miss McLemore."

Uncle Charlie clanged the dinner bell and the three gathered on the porch to eat. "This looks wonderful, Uncle Charlie! You must be expectin' more folks out here."

"Naw, just us, but it shor is a help, the supplies ya brung out, Betsy girl." It never crossed Joe's mind to bring groceries with him. From that point on though, Joe would bring plenty of provisions on his workdays at the ranch. Uncle Charlie poured sweet tea, looking a bit preoccupied. "I been thinkin', speakin' of havin' more folks, wonder if we couldn't somehow bring Josh out here for a day. Like in a wagon or somethin'?"

Betsy and Joe looked at each other. "That's a great idea, Charlie!" We could make him comfortable right here on the porch. Maybe Sunday?"

"It would be wonderful for him," Betsy said. "Mama would love it too. If it's agreeable with Doc Cartwright, let's do it."

From then on, they brought Josh out every Sunday, just for a few hours. Joe and Betsy wouldn't work that day but observed the Lord's Day, shared a meal and had "church" right there on Uncle Charlie's porch. Charlie had a well-worn Bible and Sloan brought a hymnbook she'd borrowed from Baker Baptist. Mother and daughter sang beautifully, in perfect harmony. The men? Well, they tried. After they had prayed, thanking God for his many blessings and placing a healing hand on Josh, Uncle Charlie broke in to his own hymn. "In the Sweet Bye and Bye, gimme some pie. We will meet on that beautiful shore. Gimme some more."

Everyone laughed until Sloan finally presented a fresh-baked huckleberry pie.

───

The arrival of the boy's letter in Thatcher Springs nearly caused a riot. Kate and Millie read it first at Millie's kitchen table. They were astonished the boys had met up with Kate's uncle Charlie. "If that don't beat all!" Millie exclaimed.

Kate was sniffling. "I know it's good for them. For Josh and Joe to be on their own." She blew her nose. "Right?" she asked weakly. "Sometimes I wish they were nine again. I miss them so much."

"Me too, honey. Me too." Now Millie was sniffling. "Here, Katy, take the letter on home for Max ta read. We'll share it with the others after supper."

Millie called a meeting and quickly planned a party. The whole town was ecstatic with the good news from Josh and Joey. And flabbergasted they had happened on Uncle Charlie. What a wonder. That evening they gathered in the dining room for a special dessert and Max read the letter aloud. The men got a big kick out of it. The women, of course, cried.

Little Louie Montague raised his hand at the end of the reading. "Yes, Louie?" Max asked, wondering what the youngster had to say.

"I have a idea. How 'bout every one of us writes a letter to Josh and Joey? And send them altogether in one big bundle."

Millie stood clapping. "That's a downright perfect idea, Louie! Everyone agree?" Before they could answer, she said, "Great. Please turn your letters in to me by day after tomorrow." She was giddy as a schoolgirl. It was so good to know her twinners were safe and happy.

# Chapter 5

Charlie crawled out of bed at daybreak, determined to find his dogs. It was curious that they didn't show up for supper last night. He had searched, hollering for them until dark. Surely, he'd find them today. He pulled on his boots, grabbed a cup of coffee, and started out on foot.

The path leading into the woods seemed littered with rags. As he drew closer, Charlie recognized it was pieces of deer hide. For a few minutes, he thought maybe his dogs had killed a deer, but the hide had already been tanned. *What in tarnation? Couldn't be they stole it from the neighbors. Ain't no neighbors.* All of a sudden, he heard them far ahead. "Sarge? Sarge!" he shouted. "You crazy good fer nothin' hound dogs, git on over here." He had named them both Sarge, for the sake of convenience. "C'mon, now." The two were overly excited, for being the lazy type, jumping and howling as if Charlie had been the one missing.

Once they gobbled up last night's dinner, fortunate that raccoons hadn't beat them to it, they both fell into an exhausted sleep. After chores, Charlie locked the two Sarges in the barn and took off on his horse. He was determined to get to the bottom of where that deer hide came from.

The trail took him several miles to the edge of a canyon, which didn't prove a thing. His old eyes scanned the hills across the deep ravine. Nothing. Just as he was about to turn his horse toward home, he caught movement up by the abandoned mine. Charlie dug around in his saddlebag until he found an old telescope, given him by a retired Union Army officer back when he and his brother were riding the trail to Oregon. It was more a keepsake, made of brass. He was able after a few tries to get the thing focused and finally landed on the target. It brought a fuzzy image of the entrance to an old mercury mine. But it was clear enough to pick out three horses tied there. Into the lens came a fourth horse being led by a man.

Charlie put a few landmarks to memory and headed back to the ranch, an uneasy feeling in his gut.

————

Joe worked on fence Thursday, Friday, and Saturday without Betsy, counting the hours until Sunday when the family would ride out. He put in long hours on the fence mostly to impress Betsy, he admitted to himself, but also the satisfaction of accomplishment.

Charlie was in a quandary whether or not to share his suspicion with Joe. The more he thought on it, the more he was convinced that it was the four bank robbers holed up at the old deserted mine. After praying earnestly, he concluded to wait until closer to Sunday. He feared the young man would go after them singlehandedly. Charlie planned to send a message, to notify the sheriff, with Betsy Sunday evening.

Saturday, Charlie clanged the supper bell early. Joe didn't want to quit, but he was tired and hungry, hot, and thirsty. Reluctantly he picked up his tools and headed for the house. He had to admit, Uncle Charlie's chicken and dumplings hit the spot. The two men sat on the porch after supper, drinking sweet tea, relaxing. "That was a fine meal, Uncle Charlie. Thank ya. A lotta daylight left, but sittin' here a spell feels real good."

They talked a while, Charlie convincing Joe to call it a day. "Tomorrow yer brother'll be here, and that sweet Betsy. And I'll lay odds Sloan is bakin' a big ol' pie right now! We gotta rest up. Get ready for more eatin'," Charlie laughed. There was a comfortable silence between them, and then Charlie leaned in a bit and said, "I know where they's hidin', Joe. The bank robbers."

Joe sat up, eyes wide, as he turned to face Charlie. "Are ya certain? Did ya see 'em?" Joe's heart was pounding in his ears, adrenalin rushing. "Where are they? Can we get there tonight?"

"Now hold on, son. We gotta do this right. Betsy can get word to the sheriff Sunday evenin', have a posse out here first thing Monday."

Joe could hardly sit there and wait five minutes, let alone wait until Monday. "Just tell me what you found, where they're hidin'."

Charlie told it all. How his hound dogs took off, the deer hide they'd evidently dragged all the way from the old mercury mine, down through the canyon, up the other side, leaving a trail. How Charlie would never have spotted them without his old brass scope. "Course there's no provin' it. I saw four horses. Must be four riders. Nobody in their right mind would step foot in that old decrepit mine, less they's hidin' out."

Needing to do something, Joe jumped up so abruptly that Sarge and Sarge startled awake. He bounded off the porch and marched toward the barn. Charlie slowly stood. *Oh Lord, don't let him do anything foolish.*

Joe hadn't gone to saddle his horse and load his gun as Charlie had feared but instead trekked back to the house carrying an armload of tools. Without a word, he commenced to rip off the broken steps leading to the porch.

Charlie scratched his head, perplexed, but then got the notion to pull off the hanging shutters. By dark, they had the front of the place looking much better. Just as they were ready to call it quits, Joe started tugging at the screen door. "Now son, you're just invitin' flies if ya take off that there screen door." Just then the two Sarges walked right through it, into the house.

Sloan was delighted over how good the place looked, as they drove up Sunday morning. Joe had tossed away a worn-out rug and

26

swept the porch clean, making a mental note to measure for a new screen door and purchase a rug at the mercantile in town. It had felt good throwing his energy into fixing and cleaning. His older brother Max had taught the boys at an early age, "If ya got the urge to fight, go fix somethin instead!"

After their Sunday front porch church and dinner, Joe asked Betsy if she'd like to take a walk to see how the fence was coming. They strolled along hand in hand, walking the fence line Joe had just completed. "I'm flabbergasted!" she exclaimed. "You got all this accomplished without your right-hand woman?" She laughed, but at the same time tears glistened in her blue eyes. "Mama will be so happy. Just seein' the front porch today gave her a lift. I could tell. Thank you, Joe."

Out of the blue, Joe stopped, turning to face her. "Uncle Charlie discovered their hidin' place. Those lowdown bank robbers are holed up in an old mine within ten miles of here." Joe wasn't sure how she would react.

She stared at him for a minute, soaking it in. Her expression switched to all business. "When do we go after 'em?" She was dead serious.

Now it was Joe who was flabbergasted. He pulled her into his arms. "Sweetheart," he said tenderly, "*we* are not goin' after them. I don't want you anywhere near 'em." He couldn't believe this beautiful little thing in his arms had so much courage.

When they returned to the house, Betsy spoke a few words to Charlie and disappeared inside. After several minutes, she came out with two six shooters holstered to a belt slung around her hips. "Let's take another walk, Joe."

Up behind the barn, it appeared there was a hundred miles more of broke down fence waiting to be mended. Joe didn't even want to think about it. Betsy marched ahead of him to a spot where six posts remained, more or less upright. He watched as she gathered an armload of rusty tin cans from the ground around the area. *Is she gettin' ready ta do what I think she's gonna do?* Carefully she placed a can on each of the posts.

"C'mon, Joe! Let's walk out." Betsy marched confidently away from the targets, farther and farther. "C'mon!" she hollered, motioning him to keep coming.

When they were a good distance, she turned, gave him a sweet smile, and drew both pistols. Bam! Bam! Bam! Bam! Bam! Bam! In split-second timing, she hit her targets square, using both guns. "Wanta turn?"

Joe was back to being flabbergasted again. "Betsy girl, that's the best shootin' I ever saw, bar none. Male or female. You have made your point. But no way would I put you in that kinda danger."

Everyone was quiet on the ride home, each to his own thoughts. Betsy was put out that she wouldn't be in on the ambush they had planned. As Uncle Charlie and Joe laid out their strategy, with the ladies' input, no one had seemed to notice Josh grew quiet, distant. It wrangled him that he was helpless to fight his own cause. Joe and Charlie would be risking *their* lives in retaliation for *his*. As he lay in the back of the wagon bouncing along the road home, he couldn't keep from sinking deeper into the pit of despair. He wanted to hold on to the hope everyone claimed for him. It just wasn't working. He would never walk again. Long-held tears streaked the dust on his face.

# Chapter 6

Once Sloan had the buffet set up for guests, she brought a breakfast tray to Josh and crumpled into the chair next to his bed. Both were preoccupied with what might be going on in the rugged country out back of the ranch. Betsy had tracked down Sheriff Stevens the minute they had gotten into town last night. He and his posse headed out at daybreak.

Josh had no appetite. After a long silence, he spoke, mostly to the ceiling. "I couldn't bear it if I lost my brother. He is a part of me; we're part of each other. Without Joey, I couldn't go on."

The room was quiet, somber. Sloan's voice was shaky when she finally said, "We have to trust God, Josh. That's all there is to it. Don't borrow trouble. I'm scared too—worried about Joe and Uncle Charlie. Scared for Betsy. She loves your brother." She reached for his hand. "Let's pray."

"Heavenly Father." Sloan took a deep breath. "Lord, please, please." She couldn't continue. Her heart was breaking for Betsy and the twin sister she never knew. *Oh God, please help us all.*

After a bit, Sloan said an amen, wiped her eyes, and stood abruptly. "I've got bread dough waitin'."

Josh watched from his bed into the kitchen as she kneaded dough on the worktable. He sensed there was more going on; Sloan seemed deeply disturbed. He hadn't meant to pull her into his own depression. He hadn't meant to add to her burdens. He made an attempt to lighten the gloom that hovered over both of them. He spoke into the kitchen, trying to convey optimism he didn't feel. "Joe told me how your daughter could shoot. Said she blew six cans off six fence posts in record time. Both pistols!"

Sloan had her back to him now. "Charlie taught her. He said a girl on her own should know how to protect herself." She spoke without much feeling and kept kneading.

"Well, as I've said before, Joe is one lucky cowboy ta be courtin' a girl like Betsy! I just wish there was another one like her." Josh was simply making conversation, but truly he did wish there was another one like her.

Her kneading stopped. Her shoulders froze in place. From the back, he couldn't read her expression, but her body language conveyed he'd hit a nerve. She answered so quietly he almost didn't catch it. "There is."

---

They had agreed on a plan, riding out early. There were five of them: Sherriff Stevens, two deputies, Uncle Charlie and Joe. Recalling a time when he and Josh were about twelve gave Joe an idea—a strategy. Instead of riding up to the mine where they would be visible, they would spread out wide, circle around the hideout, and come in from above. It had been Cody's idea back when the boys were playing "outlaws" with the Montagues. Once in place above their target, they would then throw rocks down past the mine as far as possible, causing a distraction.

They rode about seven miles from the ranch, before reaching the point of ambush. Joe, on his belly, looked down below to the entrance of the old mine, expecting at least to see horses. It was quiet, no horses, no signs of life. He tossed a rock and then another, creating a rustling in the brush below. Still nothing. After Sheriff Stevens sent his deputies down to get a closer look, it was clear. The no-accounts had taken off. Deputy Jones reported all manner of sign that they had been holed up there, listing the debris while pulling ticks off his neck. "The good news, tracks are fresh. Ain't been gone too long. Should be able to catch up to 'em if we can pick our way down to the trail."

It was long and tedious going, but they tracked the four horses to a stream where they lost them. Charlie and Joe walked their horses along the shallow river going upstream, while the other men went downstream keeping alert, watching for tracks leading out of the river. The sun was growing low when Joe finally spotted tracks on the south side of the river. "Over here, Charlie. They came out here." He pointed, careful not to disturb the hoofprints with his own horse.

Charlie eased up next to him, his keen eyes studying the muddy prints. After a few minutes, Uncle Charlie declared, "Only one horse came outa here, Joe. Three kept goin'. Or maybe theys went the other way. One upstream, three down. Maybe split up ta throw us off. Only one horse here."

Sure as the world the Sherriff's men had discovered the same thing in the other direction. The four outlaws had split up.

———

Sloan divided the bread dough into six loaf pans, covering them with a cloth. She wiped her hands on her apron and walked slowly into Josh's room. Her face was pale and drawn, her steps as heavy as her heart, with brokenness.

"What is it, ma'am?" He was almost afraid of the answer.

She pulled the rocker around to face him squarely. She swallowed. "There is Josh. There is another one just like Betsy. Betsy has a twin." Her eyes pooled, but she held her emotions at bay. Biting her lower lip, she took some deep breaths. "Her sister lives in New York. They have never met, have not been together since they were nine days old."

Josh was stunned as she continued on, sharing for the first time the truth. She told him everything, the way she and Alecia had both prayed all night. Because Sloan was a young widow, with no means to keep up the ranch, it was intended for both girls to be adopted. But after an agonizing night of prayer, Alecia believed it was God's will for her and Edward to adopt only one. "I will never forget that early morning when I discovered little Betsy."

"They must meet," Josh said quietly. "They have a right to know each other."

"It's been seventeen years, Josh. I feel so guilty for what I've robbed them of. I can never make it right. It's been too long." She swiped tears spilling over, determined not to cry. If she let herself cry, she may never stop. "I had detached myself from the truth of it. But you and Joe showin' up here, everything that's happened, the way you love and respect each other, the way you read each other and laugh over a shared joke or a common experience." She couldn't hold back. Sloan let the tears fall until she was sobbing.

Josh reached his hand to her shoulder. "It's not too late, Miss Sloan. I promise you, if it was me and Joe separated at birth and somebody brought us together—" Josh had to pause because of his own emotion. "If it was me and Joey, believe me we'd make up for lost time no matter how long we'd been apart. With all due respect, ma'am, you gotta write a letter to New York. Bring Betsy's sister to Oregon, her birthplace.

Sloan agonized over the decision whether or not she should write Alecia. She prayed and tried to give it over to God. She pictured leaving the whole mess at the foot of the cross, walking away with clear direction. Josh's words—"She has a right to know"—would not let her rest.

By midnight, Sloan had composed the letter. It had taken a dozen attempts, sitting at the kitchen table in the glow of a single lamp, writing and then tossing the pages away. It was impossible to convey her heart on a piece of paper. In the end, she gave up trying and simply invited Britta to visit her kinfolks in Oregon.

Sloan took the letter to town the next day, intending to post it on her way to visit the sheriff's office. Perhaps there would be an update on the pursuit of the bank robbers. She also needed to place an order with Mr. Henderson at the mercantile and return some books to the library.

When she got back to the boardinghouse in the afternoon, the letter was still in her coat pocket. "I got cold feet," she explained to Josh. "Once I leave it with the postmaster, there's no turning back. So many lives would be changed. I just can't do it."

# Chapter 7

Josh awoke suddenly to the sound of soft snoring. Just as he was trying to figure out what was going on, the grandfather clock in the parlor gonged four times. He fumbled to get the lamp lit. To his astonishment, sagged in the rocker next to his bed was an aged lady dressed in a lovely blue suit, with a matching poof of a hat atop her nodding head. *What in the world?* He stared at her, not knowing what to do.

After what seemed like an hour, the woman snorted herself awake. She looked around and then broke in to a chuckle. "Oh my. Is it time yet?" She leaned to look out the window. Josh had no idea what they were looking for but helped facilitate by pulling the curtain back. "It's still dark, Mr. Reed. We must wait a bit longer." She clasped her gloved hands together, her face beaming in the lamplight.

"You know my name?" Josh was beginning to think the woman was some kind of elderly angel.

"Why yes! Everyone knows your name. You're a hero in this town, taking a bullet to protect Mrs. Smith and her dear baby." Suddenly she looked disturbed. "On my! Please forgive my manners." She graciously held out her hand. "I'm Mrs. Eula Mae Witherspoon." Before he could say, "Glad ta meetcha," she continued. "I've just moved here. To the boardinghouse. Well, it was the split-pea soup that caught afire. Blackened most the kitchen and the whole place smells like smoke. Oh my." She shook her head and then with a big smile, her eyes sparkling, "I think it's almost time, Mr. Reed!" Abruptly she stood, leaning across Josh and looking out the window again.

"Uh Mrs. Witherspoon, what are we waiting for? And ma'am, just call me Josh. Everybody does."

"Well then, Josh, we are waiting for the sunrise! It's God's gift to us. A new day! Quick, look there!" The faintest pink bordered the tree line in the distance and then grew brighter into a deep, rich crimson, shooting beams of gold, almost blinding. "Oh my. Isn't it exquisite? Thank you, Lord Jesus, and good morning to you too!"

Sloan burst through the door, followed by a young boy. "Eula Mae? We've been lookin' all over for you, dear." She tried to sound tolerant.

"We were worried about you, Grandmother," said the boy. "Besides, Mr. Reed needs his rest."

Josh couldn't help but come to her defense. "Y'all shoulda seen the sunrise," he said as he winked at Eula Mae. "God told us good-mornin' in a most spectacular way!" The old gal winked back.

Sloan helped Mrs. Witherspoon up from the rocker and put a steadying arm around her. "Let's get you back to your room, sweetie. Get a little more rest." The boy lingered next to Josh's bed.

Eula Mae stopped at the doorway and called over her shoulder, "Jackson dear, run to the house today and bring Pastor Witherspoon's chair. The chair with wheels."

"Yes, ma'am."

Josh looked at the young man, well groomed, especially for so early in the morning. He didn't seem in any hurry to leave. "I gather you're Mrs. Witherspoon's grandson? Jackson, is it?" He reached to shake the boy's hand.

"Yes, sir, Mr. Reed. It's an honor to meet you, sir." Josh had momentarily forgotten he was the *town hero*.

Jackson broke into a huge smile when Josh invited him to stay for breakfast, so they could get to know each other.

———

Jackson Witherspoon never knew his parents. They both died of cholera on the wagon train to Oregon. His grandfather had told how they had had to unload the cook stove in order to lighten their load at one crossing, and then the oak dining table at another. "We lost over half our belongings," he had often said, "but nothing mattered. Nothing compared to the loss when we had to leave our beautiful daughter and her fine husband, buried along the trail." Then he would add, to lighten the grief, "But praise the Lord, we arrived here with *you,* Jackson. And," he would add with a twinkle in his eye, "Mother somehow got here with her seventeen gowns! Three trunks full of fluff arrived in perfect condition."

As a young woman, Eula Mae had been an expert dressmaker in Philadelphia. Her talent was in high demand among ladies of social status and wives of dignitaries. Many times those Philadelphia ladies wouldn't dream of wearing the same dress twice, so they would trade them back to her for a concession on the next one. In her limited spare time, she altered them to fit herself, although she and Pastor Witherspoon never attended a gala affair.

"So your grandfather was a pastor then?" Josh asked.

"Oh no. Grandmother just liked to call him that because she considered him such a godly man. He was a furniture maker. I think it didn't set well that they left his custom dining table on the trail." He laughed inwardly. "He made fine furniture right up until the day he died—nearly two years ago now, when I was eight."

"I'm sure he was very proud of you, Jack. You're a fine young man." He quickly added, "Is that all right? If I call ya Jack? I'd like it if you call me Josh."

From that day on, ten-year-old Jack became like a little brother to Josh. He could see how the boy needed a man in his life, especially after he learned the boy's grandmother was teaching him to crochet! "She tries to fill in for Grandfather as best she can. Grandfather used to take me fishing every Saturday. After he died, Grandmother continued the custom, at least until the time she spilled fish guts on the burgundy taffeta."

Josh laughed out loud. "Not on the burgundy taffeta! What did she say about that?"

Jack tried to stifle his own amusement. "You won't believe what she said. I'm quite sure it's the wickedest word Grandmother has even spoken." He clamped a hand over his mouth, smothering his laughter just thinking about it.

"Tell me. What did she say? 'Fiddle dee-dee?'"

"It was worse than that. She said—" Jack couldn't quit giggling. "She said, 'Oh shucky-doo!'"

Josh hadn't laughed that hard in a long time. The two unlikely companions laughed every time they looked at each other. There was a bonding that day and Josh promised himself, even if he couldn't walk, even if he felt like half a man, he was going to be the man in Jack's life.

———

Joe had been terribly worried about Josh after last Sunday at the ranch. His brother had seemed extra quiet, gloomy. He couldn't blame him for being discouraged. Joe was plenty discouraged himself, after losing track of those polecat outlaws. Riding back to Baker City, he prayed, all fourteen miles, about the whole situation. By the time he had reached the edge of town, knowing Betsy would be waiting for him, things didn't seem quite so bleak.

He noticed a commotion right in the middle the road out in front of the general store—a parade or a celebration of some kind. Youngsters were surrounding someone, laughing excitedly, and townsfolk, standing on the boardwalks, were cheering with ladies waving hankies and men saluting. As Joe slowed his horse to get a closer look, he couldn't believe his eyes. Slowly he took of his hat. "Well, bless Pat!"

It was his first outing in the wheelchair. When Jack had brought it to the boardinghouse that day, Josh was astonished at the fine craftsmanship, the perfect condition. It was polished oak, with heavy caning on the adjustable back. The leg supports were adjustable too, and the wheels, crafted by a blacksmith, were made to withstand rough roads. "Of course, Pastor Witherspoon built it," declared Eula Mae, "for me. In case I ever need it."

With Jack's encouragement, Josh decided to try it out. He knew his upper body had lost strength for lying in bed so much, not working. He would never complain about chopping wood again, if he ever got the chance to do it. He determined to give the wheelchair a try.

Before they'd reached the heart of town, two little girls ran out from one of the shops shouting, "It's Mr. Reed! Howdy, Mr. Reed!" They ran over, handing him their recently purchased bag of peppermint sticks.

Little by little, people lined the road, cheering. "Thank you, Joshua Reed! You're a hero in Baker City! We love you, Josh! God bless you, son!" Children followed behind the slow-moving wheelchair, until Josh stopped, shaking his head. Tears threatened as he tried to speak. Finally, Jack spoke on his behalf, in his deepest and loudest voice. "Mr. Reed, er Josh, is grateful for your outpouring of support and kindness. He thanks you very much."

"I couldn't have said it better myself, buddy," Josh said softly.

# Chapter 8

There was a change in Josh. He seemed happier. Joe wasn't sure if it was the wheelchair or that fact he had taken on a project in young Jack. Leaving the confines of his convalescent room and getting out into the crisp fall air he knew was part of it. While Joe was in town, he would build a ramp for the wheelchair.

It had become customary for Jack to stay and have breakfast with Josh, after "sunrise service" as they'd come to call it. Eula Mae didn't make it every day, but when she did, she came dressed to the hilt—this morning in her teal-green ensemble, peacock feathers trimming her hat. She left Josh with a Bible verse *God had given her just for him*. "You can read it later, dear," she had told him with a twinkle in her eye.

Josh and Jack chatted easily while wolfing down Sloan's flakey biscuits and gravy. They were ruminating about the wheelchair ride to town and the way folks had come out to applaud Joshua. Out of the blue, Josh asked, "You know how ta rope a steer?"

Jack glanced out the window as if there might be one in the backyard. He looked puzzled. "No, not really."

About that time, Joe walked in to see if his brother wanted to give the ramp a try.

"You bet, Joey, and I thank ya for buildin' it. I was wonderin', since ya got the tools handy, could I ask another favor? We need us a dummy steer. Jack here is gonna learn to rope!"

———

Sloan had still not mailed the letter to New York. She had made three attempts but couldn't muster the courage. *Maybe today.* She reached inside her coat pocket, where she had carried it, only to find it gone. *Did I take it out? Could it be in my handbag?* It was not there either, nor was it in the desk drawer. The letter was nowhere to be found. She became alarmed, a sense of panic threatening.

Trying to sound calm, she asked Mrs. Bush, Eula Mae, and other boarders if they had seen a letter by chance. She was about to ask Josh if he knew anything about it, when Betsy walked in, carrying a bundle of mail. She had a big smile on her face. "Joshua Reed? Looks like you and Joe have a lota fans in Thatcher Springs, Idaho! She handed him at least a dozen letters tied together with twine. "Oh, and I mailed your letter to Aunt Alecia, Mama. It was on the hallway floor." Josh watched the color drain from Sloan's face.

When she delivered Josh's dinner that evening, Sloan collapsed into the rocking chair like a rag doll. He noticed she hadn't brought dinner for herself. She just sat while Josh slowly started eating, but not with the usual gusto. He took a drink of coffee. "When ya plannin' ta tell her?" Josh inquired gently.

She let out a sigh. "I guess that would be the next thing. It's just so hard, Josh. I don't know where to begin. What to say. How to say it."

"Would it be easier if we were with ya? Me and Joe? Uncle Charlie?"

She looked doubtful. "I have a few weeks. The mail is slow-going to New York. It'll take a while. I can wait."

He ignored her struggle to put it off. "How about Sunday, Miss Sloan, out at the ranch?"

———

Sloan had not slept, rehearsing how in heaven's name she would tell Betsy. Sweet Betsy. *How can I tell her she has a twin sister? After seventeen years, Lord, how can tell her? Please help me, Lord Jesus. I can't do it. I just can't do it.*

But that Sunday, she did do it. Sitting on the porch at the ranch, she told Betsy that her "cousin" in New York was not her cousin at all but her sister. Her twin sister. Even Uncle Charlie shed a tear as Sloan sobbed her heart out with the truth she had held inside all these years. Joe was quite shaken too, feeling for Betsy. Josh reached for Sloan's hand on one side and Betsy's on the other and quietly began to pray. Joe added to it and Uncle Charlie ended it. Softly they all said amen. Except for Betsy. "I'd like to take a walk," she said, her voice strained. "Please excuse me."

Joe jumped up. "I'll go with ya, Betsy." But she shook her head, and Joe respected her wish.

They watched her climb the fence, pull herself up on Patches, no saddle, no bridle, and walk him across the rolling pasture. Joe never took his eyes off her until he could no longer see her as the dark timberland on the far side seemed to swallow her up. "I don't think she should go into the woods." Joe sat forward in his chair. "She's not in a good frame of mind."

"Give her a little time, Joe," Uncle Charlie said with a calmness he didn't feel.

———

Patches plodded along, following a deer trail. Betsy was numb, unconscious of where she was, her mind filled with the revelation *I have a sister.* She wanted to feel happy. But somehow, the pain of years lost overshadowed the joy. Thinking of Joe and Josh, their dedication to each other, the plans they made together, the fun they shared—could she have that kind of love with her sister? *Sister.* It was like a foreign word.

41

Betsy was unaware how deeply she had ventured into the forest. Patches stopped; his ears perked up as if a wild animal was nearby. She scanned the area for a deer or coyote. Nothing. For the first time, Betsy realized she had gone too far and had best go back. Patches continued to act strangely. Just as she grasped his mane to turn him back, the rustle of brush and sound of snapping limbs drew her eyes a few paces into the face of a filthy heavily bearded man, horseback. Right before Betsy kicked her horse into action, she noticed a deep scar across his left eyebrow.

Leaning low over Patches, she ran him as best she could through heavy woods, leaping over fallen logs. A rifle shot rang out, just missing her, but when she turned to see how close he was, a low branch scraped her clean off her horse. Betsy was stunned, disoriented as the outlaw yanked her up, swiftly tying her hands together with a dirty rope.

———

Joe was getting worried. "I'm going after her." Just then her riderless horse broke out of the timber and onto the meadow, running full out for home. *Oh dear God!*

Sloan didn't wait for anyone to object but took Charlie's horse and followed Joe. It was an unspoken understanding that Uncle Charlie would stay with Josh.

The two raced through the meadow, following the way Betsy had gone, but when they got deep into the woods with no sign of her, fear gripped both hearts.

"Maybe we should fan out, one go that way and—"

Joe cut her off. "No, Sloan. We stay together."

As they urged their horses through the brush and bramble, searching for tracks, finally Joe spotted what appeared to be Patches' tracks and followed to a point he could tell she turned abruptly, eventually coming to the place where she had hit the ground. There appeared another set of tracks. A different horse.

———

"Yer a purty little thing." The outlaw spit a stream of tobacco juice.

Betsy was trying to determine where they were. Her hands were bound in front of her, which to her way of thinking was a mistake for the lowdown varmint holding her captive. After what seemed like hours, Betsy shifted a bit, trying to get comfortable on the rocky ground. "Ya might as well relax, girlie. We ain't makin' a move till sundown. You're gonna be helpin' me go after the loot." He laughed harshly. "What d'ya think a that, blondie?"

She didn't answer or even look at him. He kept jawing away. She ignored him. "What's a matter? Cat got yer tongue?" He laughed again and spit, just missing her boot. "Got nothin ta say?"

"I'm busy talkin' ta God," she declared, which brought a fit of laughter to her captor, throwing him into a coughing spell. He took a swig from his moonshine jug.

"Well, don't bother yerself tellin' God about me. We ain't got nothin ta do with each other."

Betsy looked disgusted. "Don't flatter yourself." Even in the predicament she was in, Betsy could only think about the reality that she had a sister. At first, she had been hurt that something of such significance had been kept from her for all those years. But riding across the pasture, she realized something significant had been kept from Britta too. A picture came to her mind of what must have been the heartbreaking moment her mother, a young widow, had made such a painful decision. An unselfish choice, for what she believed best for her children. *Lord, please help me accept this news with grace. Help me receive my sister Britta. Forgive me for harboring resentment toward Mama.*

Deep snoring startled Betsy back to the present. The mangy outlaw was asleep. She was stiff from sitting in the same position so long, but without a sound, she got to her feet. The rock she had eyed earlier was a step toward her captor. His rifle lay across his lap, his chin on his chest as he dozed. With her hands still tied at the wrists, she bent to pick up the rock. He snorted awake, but not in time. He never knew what hit him.

Joe and Sloan were a good distance, but when Betsy scrambled out of the shallow ditch where she was being held, Joe spotted her, a shaft of sun shining on her golden hair. He leaped off his horse before it even stopped and pulled Betsy into his arms.

Now that she was found, she burst into tears. "I knew you'd come, Joe," she sobbed.

Sloan pulled her horse to a stop just behind Joe, jumping down to embrace her daughter at the same time. "Let's untie your hands, sweetheart. Who did this? Did they hurt you?" She looked around cautiously.

Joe helped Betsy up on his horse. He would get the women to safety and then deal with whoever was out there. "Let's get her home."

# Chapter 9

"Well, Jack, are ya ready? I say it's a fine day ta rope a steer!" Josh declared from his wheelchair, which he had easily maneuvered down the new ramp, into the backyard of the boardinghouse.

Jack was all smiles, especially after Joe had donated the use of his sweat-stained, frumpy cowboy hat. "I'll see ya get one of yer own," he had promised, "but this here hat's seen a lot a steer ropin'. You can wear it for good luck."

The dummy steer was a sawhorse with a sun-bleached skull the Reed boys had picked up, a souvenir of their adventure to Oregon. "Before ever tryin' ta rope a real live steer, from a real live horse ya need to master this here little fella from the ground. It can be real dangerous otherwise. My pa got his thumb pinched off, after one ol' ornery critter jerked the slack out of his rope. Happened so fast, he didn't know it at first. So best pay attention ta what I say."

"Yes, sir!" replied Jack. He was excited just to rope the dummy, let alone a real steer.

"First, let's build a loop. See this little ring at the end? It's called a honda. Go ahead and grab hold of it, and slide some rope through."

Jack complied, biting down on his tongue with concentration.

"Once the loop is about this big," Josh indicated, "flip it over and slide it back some more. You'll have better control and accuracy if you build a decent-sized loop. To swing it, ya can't hold to the honda, so grab it with your left hand and pull some extra rope out of your coils, about the length of your arm. That part is your spoke." Jack was being careful to follow instruction. "Good job, Jack! Ready ta rope that ol' steer?"

"I think so. Where do I stand?"

"Right back here, a little to the left. And use your arm, not your wrist when ya swing your loop. Here, watch me." From his wheelchair, Josh went through each step, though it felt awkward not being on his feet. "Watch my loop turn over in front of me. The tip is down over my left shoulder and up over my right. Ya ready?"

Jack had managed to rope everything but the steer, taking out a section of prized rose bushes that had made it all the way from Missouri. With the rope out of control, Jack had knocked over the garden tools leaning against the shed, the wash board which had been leaning against the tub, and Josh's hat clean off his head. He had pretty much "roped" everything except the dummy steer. When at last he roped Mrs. Bush's bloomers from the clothesline, he turned with slumped shoulders and looked at Josh—defeat written all over his face. "Oh, shucky-doo," they said in unison.

The next day went better, which was good because Jack's grandmother sat in the porch swing to watch. "Oh my. How lovely, Jackson. You're coming ever so close!"

Josh called him over. "Now Jack, remember everything I told ya, buddy. Act like ya own it!"

Jackson walked back out, prepared the rope just like Josh said, and took a deep breath. With wild abandon, he let her fly. The crowd, which now included Sloan and Mrs. Bush, cheered and clapped. "Ya did it, Jack! Ya did it!" Josh was so proud he wanted to jump up and down. If only he could.

That night Josh looked up the scripture verse Eula May had encouraged him to read.

> The Lord gives strength to the weary and increases
> the power of the weak. Even youths grow tired and

weary and young men stumble and fall; but those who hope in the Lord will renew their strength. They will soar on wings like eagles; they will run and not grow weary, they will walk and not be faint. (Isaiah 40:29–31)

"Those who hope in the Lord will walk!" Josh said out loud. Then he bowed his head and prayed.

———

Betsy was almost glad to be back working at the café. The busyness helped keep her mind off everything that happened last Sunday. It had settled on her how bad things could have been, being abducted by a fugitive, out in the deep woods. After her description, Joe was sure it was one of the bank robbers.

"Did he have any scars? Maybe on his forehead?" Joe had asked.

"Well, yes," she answered. "He started out with one." And with a snicker, "Now he's got two."

Joe had been too worried about Betsy to go looking for the outlaw, but he kept thinking about what he'd said, about Betsy helping him "go after the loot." He wondered how Betsy could help him. He didn't see how she could be much help, unless the loot was stashed somewhere in town.

———

Eula Mae had asked Jackson to run down to the house that afternoon, with a list of items she needed. "Mind if I come along? Now that I have my own transportation, I'd like ta see where y'all lived."

"Yes, sir!" Jack replied with new enthusiasm for the errand. "The house has even got a ramp. Grandfather thought of everything."

It was a longer trip than he expected, but Josh savored the outdoors. He breathed in deeply of the cool air. *Thank ya, Lord. I've taken so much for granted.*

The Witherspoon home was situated at the edge of town, on a five-acre parcel that butted up to a hillside, continuing into timberland. It was a lovely two-story Victorian-style home. "This place looks just like your grandmother."

Once inside, Josh thought even more so. Despite the smell of burned pea soup, it was elegant, the furnishings ornate. Josh sat contently, taking it all in while Jack went to gather his grandmother's things. They would have to hurry now as daylight was fading.

He wasn't gone two minutes when Jack came back into the parlor with an uneasy look on his face. He glanced around like he was worried. "What's wrong?" Josh asked.

"Something's not right. Someone's been here. In Grandfather's library."

Josh wheeled the chair that direction, as Jack pointed out things that were a bit out of place. "This rug, the corner is turned up like somebody stumbled on it. And Grandfather's books were stacked in a certain way. Not like this." As if something occurred to him suddenly, he looked over his shoulder at the portrait behind his grandfather's desk. Josh followed his eyes. A large gilded framed painting of George Washington was the focal point of the stately room. They looked knowingly at each other. It had been moved.

"Grandfather's safe is behind George Washington," the boy said. "Somebody's been here."

Standing on the leather seat of his grandfather's desk chair, Jack carefully "opened" the hinged portrait, exposing a wall safe. It was still locked. "Grandmother can't remember the combination, so everything is still in it. Probably take a stick of dynamite to get it open."

Even though Josh was mostly helpless, he was sure glad Jack had not gone down there by himself. "Go ahead and gather up the stuff for Mrs. Witherspoon and let's skedaddle. Leave everything just the way we found it, corner of the rug and all."

Joe had gone back out to McLemore Ranch, trying to push completion of the last stretch of fence before winter set in. He was determined to see cows grazing in the front pasture, come spring. He was also determined to stay after the hooligan that shot his brother. Josh confided in Betsy about the discovery at Mrs. Witherspoon's home. "It's just a gut feelin', but we think somebody's comin' in there at night. It's obvious the house is sittin' empty. Tomorrow night, me and Jack are gonna stake out the place, spend the night. I just thought somebody should know. Don't want Sloan or Jack's grandmother to worry none. We're tellin' 'em we're takin' a "campin' trip" down at the house."

"Are you sure that's a good idea? You and Jack could be outnumbered and"—she glanced at Josh's unmoving legs under the covers—"overpowered."

Jack's grandfather had cleverly built a secret closet—more like a small room—behind the built-in bookcases in his library. A section could be slid open where they were sure the wheelchair would fit through, for a perfect hideout. Once they were situated, they would slide the section closed from behind, leaving a tiny gap to spy on intruders that might show up.

---

The boardinghouse was quiet, everyone in bed for the night, except for Betsy. She couldn't sleep, so she slipped down to the kitchen to make a cup of cocoa. It was nice just to sit by the remaining embers in the cook stove, to think and to pray. She was still having doubts about meeting Britta. Her sister. *I can't get over it, Lord. Me. Betsy McLemore. I have a twin sister!* Footsteps in the hallway drew her attention. She turned to see Eula Mae. "Can I help ya, ma'am?"

"Well, dear, Jackson forgot his pajamas! The nights are getting rather cold. Thought I'd take them to him."

"It's nearly midnight! How did ya think you'd get down to the house, ma'am?" They were both speaking just above a whisper so as not to wake the house.

"Oh my." Her eyebrows knitted together as though it hadn't crossed her mind. "Perhaps you could go too, Betsy dear. Hitch up the buggy? Have you noticed the bright harvest moon?"

Betsy nearly laughed out loud, until the thought came to her that Eula Mae might be on to something. She would love an excuse to check on Josh and Jack. "Well, let me get my coat and gather up some blankets."

Other than a few gas lamps and of course the silvery moonlight, the saloon was the only establishment radiating lights and sounds of honky-tonk music along the dark street. A horse and rider appeared from the alley, startling Betsy. Eula Mae recognized him. "Hello, Sheriff Stevens! Oh my. What a lovely evening."

The sheriff thought it strange, the two ladies out after dark, unaccompanied. "Everything all right, Miss Betsy?"

"We're just goin' down to the Witherspoon place, Sheriff, check on Jack and Josh." She winked, hoping the sheriff would read between the lines. He didn't.

"Mainly we're taking Jack his pajamas," explained Eula Mae. "The boys are having a campout. Isn't that lovely?"

"Well then, if everything is all right, I'll go ahead and make my rounds." He tipped his hat. "Evenin', ladies."

In the light of the moon, the two-story Victorian looked eerie, the trees casting shadows. The house was completely dark inside. Betsy suggested Eula Mae stay snugged up in the buggy while she went in to fetch Jack. "I'll have him come out ta get his pajamas and say hello."

The older lady was so enraptured by the big moon, she was perfectly content and not in the least afraid. Betsy climbed the stairway to the porch, completely engulfed in dark shadows. Before she could tap on the door, a rough hand clamped over her mouth and an arm grabbed her around the waist. She recognized the stench.

Her captor kicked open the door. "Well, well. I guess you're gonna help me after all, blondie." He laughed harshly, tying her hands behind her back this time. He'd learned a lesson, still plagued by headaches from the rock episode. Betsy struggled, but to no avail.

Josh and Jack were in position, behind the secret door in the library. They could hear a commotion in the parlor but had no idea it involved Betsy. The moonlight cast its glow through tall library windows. When the outlaw walked in yanking his bound and gagged prisoner with him, he lit the lamp on the desk, making their target much more visible.

It took all Josh had not to shout out Betsy's name as he watched her treated roughly, helpless to do anything. He had his rifle aimed through the opening of the shelves. Jack had his peashooter. Josh kept hidden as he shouted loudly, "Let her go! We've got ya covered!"

The outlaw pulled Betsy in front of him like a shield, looking around wildly for where the voice had come from. He wondered how many of them were somewhere in that room. "Wouldn't bother me a bit ta put a bullet in this purty blonde head."

It all erupted when Jack shot a pea that pinged off the lamp and another off the outlaw's nose. Betsy was in his grasp with hands tied, but her feet were free. She took advantage of the distraction to kick the heel of her boot furiously into the man's leg. He let out a yelp and a few expletives, letting his hold on her slip. At that moment, glass shattered from the window opposite the wall of books, where Josh and Jack were hiding. Sheriff Stevens announced his arrival. "It's over, ya no-account yella-bellied back shooter. Drop yer firearm! Pronto!" At that very moment, another figure appeared in the doorway.

"Grandmother?" Eula Mae stood unwavering, aiming a double-barreled shotgun directly at the outlaw's belly.

"Put your hands in the air this very instant, you, you yellow-bellied skunk!"

# Chapter 10

Back in Thatcher Springs, Millie was grateful that even though the stage coach rarely stopped anymore, things were busy in the little settlement. With the new bank and several new establishments, the town was buzzing, the hub for ranch families in outlying areas.

Clay Johnson, a talented saddlemaker, had joined forces with Pierre and Simone, adding on to their leather shop. They had established a shipping service of their goods, taking advantage of the railroad stop within forty miles. Clay fit right in with the Montague family, and it was obvious he was smitten with Margot. Margot thought Clay was very handsome and laughed at everything he said.

The Montague boys had grown like weeds. Andre had become partner with his father in the fur trade, trapping together much of the time, although he went out on his own more and more, while Pierre worked in the shop. Louis was considering going to school back east, maybe learn a trade. He excelled in all areas of study. He was Grace's best student.

Wade McKenzie became full-time preacher of God's House, the result mainly of Kitty staying on in Thatcher Springs. The Penroses had invited her to live with them, after Cody and Lila's wedding, and though she was grateful, Kitty never wanted to go back to San Francisco again. Millie was delighted to hire her as hostess in the dining room and pianist on Sunday morning. For Kitty, it was the chance she needed for a new start, an added blessing that the preacher paid her so much attention.

The Reed household was full of children, their fields full of cows. Behind their log house, Kate grew a lush garden, well fenced to keep the critters out. The family would soon be digging up potatoes by the bushel. Even in their busyness, Max and Kate felt the void of Josh and Joey. It was still their custom to sit on the porch or in front of the hearth in cold weather, drinking coffee and sharing their day, often reminiscing about the boys. They were happy for them on one hand but missed them terribly.

Millie missed them too. And she missed Cody. And Lila. And she had grown so fond of Gus Carter and Pearl Alexander, Kate's sister. The two had married and, right after Josh and Joe headed for Oregon, Gus and Pearl headed to the mission field in China. The good news was it was far more exciting watching for the mail these days.

———

Everyone in Thatcher Springs noticed a twinkle in Millie's eyes of late. Silas figured she was planning a party. He walked in the kitchen early one morning to steal a cup of coffee—and a kiss. He loved her more than ever. "You need help today, darlin'? Settin' up for the meetin' tonight?"

"Thank you, dear. Kate and Grace will have it set up," she replied. "They're havin' a school program, ya know, and how I love those school programs!" Other than Bible study held once a week in the dining room, monthly town meetings and special programs were now held at the church building.

"Silas dear, sit for a minute. I need ta ask ya about somethin'." Millie smiled up at him.

*Here it comes*, he thought. "What's on yer mind, Millie?" He pulled up to the kitchen table just as she delivered two cups of hot coffee.

"I plan to make a special announcement tonight. Everyone'll be so surprised!" Her eyes sparkled, like a little girl with a peppermint stick. "It's only right you're in agreement with me. I want your blessin' on the matter first. Before I tell the others." She smiled at him and waited.

"Uh, well, go on then." *What in tarnation is this women cookin' up?*

Millie was about to bust. She'd been planning this for so long. "Well, Silas, what would ya think of—a family reunion! All of us, all of Thatcher Springs! And Josh and Joey too! And Cody and Lila!, At the ocean!" Millie was beaming like a schoolgirl.

Silas wanted to share her enthusiasm, but he thought it an impossible undertaking. Trying to sound encouraging, he asked, "Where would everyone stay, sweetheart? How would they get there? Who would watch over this here town?"

"Silas darlin', I have it all figured out. We'll close down the town for a month. I've hired a deputy sheriff and his posse to guard the shops and buildings. Sheriff Buckingham will bring his wife to cook and keep the place up and his two sons to take care of the animals. With rail service now, it'll be easy for travel, and we already have reservations on the Oregon Coast! Oh Silas! Isn't it wonderful?"

"Millie, honey. It all sounds great, but there's a lot of people in this family. I can't imagine puttin' a hold on that many rooms. It could backfire and there'd we be. Stuck. In Oregon. With all them young'uns." He was specifically thinking of Grace and Sam's boys. Silas and Millie called them "wild Indians" when the parents were out of earshot. "You for sure got bona fide reservations?"

Millie was not the least discouraged. She hopped up to get more coffee. With her back to him, she took a deep breath. "Yes, Silas, dear. The reservations are guaranteed. It's a sure thing." She turned toward him, smiling her irresistible smile. "We bought the place."

———

Joe could not get over it. He didn't know whether to be mad or glad that the bank robber that shot his brother in the back was behind bars. He was obsessed with taking him himself, to even the score. The no-good sidewinder had destroyed his brother's life. Somehow the bum had slipped his "noose" more than once, and then to think—Josh in a wheelchair, ten-year-old Jack, Betsy, and the elderly Mrs. Witherspoon had made the capture! Of course, it was a good thing the sheriff was in on it too. He had the handcuffs.

Evidently the four outlaws had gotten into a big ruckus and split up, deciding to go off in different directions. They had divided the loot, but somehow sly Clem Holiday, the one locked up in Baker City Jail, had stolen the other men's portions, leaving a bag of rocks in their three saddlebags. He had wandered into the edge of town from the forest side and discovered Witherspoon's empty house and stashed the bounty in the safe behind George Washington. Cracking safes was his specialty. It had turned out a perfect hideout, even providing hay in the barn for his horse. For all his trouble, all his conniving, the money was now back in the bank. Eventually he gave names and descriptions of the other outlaws, maybe reducing the possibility of getting strung up.

---

The weather was changing in eastern Oregon. Even though skies remained sunny and blue, the nights were becoming colder, turning aspens on the ranch a brilliant golden yellow. Jack rode out with the family, sitting in the back of the wagon with Josh. They still laughed about Eula Mae calling the bank robber a "yellow-bellied skunk." "That one's better than shucky-doo," Jack declared, and the two laughed all over again. "She asked me if her gray gabardine had been appropriate for the confrontation."

"You are blessed to have a granny like Eula Mae Witherspoon," Josh said, and he meant it. "In her own amusing way, she's made a difference in my life."

"I know what ya mean, Josh." He giggled. "Just don't ever call her 'granny' to her face though."

It was Jack's first Sunday at the ranch, but he became a regular after that. He was so excited when Betsy offered, "Go ahead, Jack. Take Patches out for a ride." He'd never really ridden on a ranch like that, out in the open, wearing Joe's cowboy hat.

Josh encouraged him. "Show 'em what ya can do with a rope!" The bunch was impressed how spot-on he had become with the dummy steer, which they had hauled out in the wagon. He secretly wished he could try it on a real steer someday.

"How 'bout you teach *us* somethin'?" Josh said. "Like how in the world ya got so good with a peashooter." Betsy went to work setting up tin cans, and from the front porch, all six were pinging peas off everything including each other. Jack was the only one to hit a can. "This is the best day I ever had," he declared, and they hadn't even had the pie yet.

Betsy jumped up to help her mother serve the pie. As they walked in the house together, she quietly said, "I think Britta will like it out here, Mama." Sloan pulled her daughter into a long hug.

———

Millie grabbed the fat envelope, hollering a thank-you to the Express rider. She couldn't wait to open it. As she spread photograph after photograph out on the kitchen table, Kate walked in.

"Oh Katy! I'm so glad you're here. The pictures just came! Come sit down with me. I'll get the coffee."

The previous owners, who were still managing the Inn at Seaside, had sent pictures at Millie's request, and several pages of descriptions. The two women poured through each one, their excitement building for the reunion. The whole town was excited about it; everyone planned to go. Millie's mind kept her awake at night, making plans. Now she had another project. "Let's redecorate!"

Much to Millie's surprise, Grace came up with the best ideas. All the women had gathered the next afternoon to discuss the possibilities. "It needs to be lighter," she said. "Maybe take down the heavy brocade draperies and hang sheer linen instead? We want to see the ocean, after all."

"Grace, that's a wonderful idea. And what do y'all think about the wallpaper?"

By the time the meeting was over, the ladies had changed everything. Millie carefully wrote out instructions to a decorating company in Portland, requesting wallpaper and drapery samples. The whole main floor, great room, and dining room would be lightened with a cream brocade wallpaper, instead of the existing dark burgundy and green. Rustic wood joists, stained dark, ran vertical about every eight feet, giving the effect of panels of wallpaper in-between.

"And what about this idea, Mother?" Grace continued. "Each section with the cream brocade would make a lovely background for artwork." Millie clapped her hands together. She not only had a perfect idea for the "artwork"—she also loved when Gracie called her *Mother*.

Silas had finally warmed up to the idea of Millie buying the place. "After all, darlin'," she had said, "what else would we do with our 'inheritance'?" She would never in all her life forget the day Cody had left the folks of Thatcher Springs generous shares of his father's gold.

# Chapter 11

The light rain felt good to Sloan for a change, as she pulled her coat tighter and headed out for errands. She felt anxious on one hand and eager on the other. Today she would visit the bank and make a payment on her delinquent mortgage. Uncle Charlie had received down payments on two saddle orders, and with that and what she and Betsy had saved, she had a total of $172.

Walking into the bank, across the marble floor where not all that long ago Josh lay wounded, brought a wave of revulsion. It was a day she'd never forget. So much had happened since the Reed brothers had come to town.

The bank president, Mr. Abernathy, greeted her with a cordial smile and ushered her into his office. Her heartbeat picked up, fearing what he might say, that the payment would barely make a dent in her debt. She swallowed. "I hope you can visit the ranch soon, Mr. Abernathy. You'd be amazed at the improvements. The front pasture is completely fenced and repairs to the house—"

"Mrs. McLemore," he interrupted, "I have something to say." He pulled open the desk drawer, retrieving an envelope.

She hurried on, fearing bad news. "Sir, I'm making a payment today of $172." She dug around in her handbag for the envelope of money. "I know it's not quite enough to—"

He interrupted again. "Sloan, the mortgage on your ranch has been paid in full."

She didn't think she'd heard right. "Excuse me? I'm planning to make another payment—"

"It's been paid off dear. Late fees, back taxes, everything. Congratulations, Sloan, you own McLemore Ranch, free and clear." He handed her the deed.

Sloan was speechless. She started to cry. "How? Who paid it?"

"Well, it's confidential dear. I'm not at liberty to say. Just appreciate the gift."

———

Sloan walked out of the bank, stunned, tears still streaming. She had to tell Betsy. The closer she got to the café, the more she picked up her pace until she was running, laughing, crying, and shouting out, "Good morning!" to curious passersby.

"What is it, Mama?" Betsy feared some kind of bad news. She sat the tray of hot meals, ready for delivery, on the nearest table, as her mother burst through the door.

Waving the envelope in her hand, Sloan exclaimed, "It's the deed to the ranch, Betsy! Someone paid it off!" A new set of tears threatened as Betsy strived to comprehend. "We own it free and clear! No more payments."

Betsy was in disbelief herself. "Who would do that? Maybe it's a mistake."

From the kitchen, the cook hollered, "Betsy! Get ta crackin' out there!" When she didn't respond, he walked with intention into the dining room. He paid no mind to Sloan's presence. "I got a notion ta give ya the boot, girlie."

Betsy untied her apron, methodically folded it, and offered it to the crabby boss. "Not necessary, sir. I'm turning in my resignation." She looped her arm through Sloan's and started toward the door. "Oh, that tray of meatloaf specials goes to table seven."

Before Sloan completed her order at the mercantile, she led Betsy to the fabric department. "Pick out whatever you like, sweetheart. I'm gonna make ya a new dress! You haven't had a decent dress in ages." She wanted her daughter to look nice when she met her *other* daughter.

Betsy claimed she didn't need a new dress but was elated when the clerk bundled the deep blue cotton material, thread, buttons, and trim. Betsy loved the color blue. "Thank you, Mama."

On the way back home, they stopped by the post office, the anticipation building as they looked for a letter from Alecia. Enough time had passed. Surely they would hear something soon. "Nothing from New York today, ma'am. But here's one for the Reed boys, if ya care ta deliver it."

---

"We'll need the sled before long." Sloan shivered as she and Betsy huddled together on the wagon seat. The temperature dropped during the night, making it a very cold ride to the ranch. Josh and Jack were in the back, nestled in a straw bed with quilts piled on. They could be heard laughing. Seemed they always had something to laugh about lately.

They had begun the cleanup process in Eula Mae's kitchen, ripping off burned planks from behind the stove, a result of the pea soup incident. At the end of yesterday, the place was in more of a mess than it had started out, and they were praying Jack's grandmother would not decide to stop by after church. "We might have ta get a bona fide carpenter to help us out, Jack, before she sees it."

Jack got the giggles. "No telling what she might call us!"

"So long as she doesn't come after us with her shotgun!" It felt like being a kid again to Josh, reminding him of growing up with his brother Joe and the mischief they got into. *Thank you, Lord for my buddy Jack. But I do miss my brother.*

The ranch house was warm and toasty as the family gathered inside for Sunday dinner. Sloan had brought out a deep pot of stew to heat up and fresh bread, and of course a pie. She couldn't wait to share the news. Once she had everyone's attention, she was unable to speak, caught up in emotion. Sloan choked up, tears spilling over. Words wouldn't come. Betsy took her hand and did the speaking. "What Mama is trying to say, the mortgage on McLemore Ranch, this place, has been paid off!" Betsy got a little teary eyed too. "Someone—they want to remain anonymous—paid the whole thing!" Mother and daughter hugged, laughing and crying.

Josh shot a glance at Joe, who winked. Jack smiled a big smile, recognizing the good news. Uncle Charlie said, "Well, I'll be jiggered! Got any ideas who done it?"

Over dinner they discussed the possibilities of who it could be that paid off the loan and discussed the plans Sloan had waited so long to complete. Come spring, she would start rebuilding a cow herd. She wanted to finish repairs to the house and eventually fix up the barn. "I'm just so thankful to the Lord. So thankful for this blessin'." She shook her head, swiping away fresh tears. "I can't get over it."

Late afternoon, Joe and Betsy bundled up for their Sunday walk. It was really the only time they had alone. Now that Betsy had quit the café, he was planning on more of it. "I'm so proud of you for stickin' with the job as long as ya did, Betsy, and always havin' a good attitude. I know ya put up with a lot in order to help yer ma."

"Mama has had so much on her plate, Joe. All these years carryin' the burden of guilt, havin' another daughter thousands of miles away. She's worked so hard without a complaint. I know she misses my father terribly. They were so young."

Joe tightened his arm around her shoulder. "Well, I'm glad somethin good finally happened for her. For both of you."

They walked a while in silence, the air cooling even more as the sun was making its descent in the west. Betsy stopped, turning toward him. "*You* did it, didn't you, Joey? You and Josh paid off the bank."

Joe chuckled, looking everywhere but at her. "What makes ya say that?"

She just stood there looking up at him, her eyes big, pooling with tears.

He pulled her to him, holding her tight. "Oh Betsy. Sweet Betsy." They held each other closely for a long minute, and then Joe gently tipped her chin until their lips met. He kissed her longingly; she kissed back. He wiped her tears away with his thumb and kissed her again. "I love you, Betsy."

# Chapter 12

Millie had written to Josh and Joe to announce the reunion. "Whew." Josh let out a low whistle. "Sure hope I'm walkin' by July." He had mixed feelings about the idea of joining his family on the Oregon Coast. He missed them all so much. But he couldn't let them see him like that—paralyzed.

The two reminisced about their family. Max was not only their older brother; he had been their sole guardian since they were seven. He was like a father to them, training the boys by his example to be hardworking, Bible-believing, upright citizens. And Kate. They loved her from day one and knew she loved them too. She was fervent in mothering—a beautiful reflection of God's love. And there was no one quite like Millie. "Remember when we interviewed her?" Josh laughed.

"And she made sure we had cookies and milk, even if they weren't baked yet! And Silas. He lived out his faith right before our eyes. Who would ever guess it all started when he kidnapped Kate!" Joe exclaimed, and both the boys shook their heads and laughed heartily.

Of course, old Henry had passed on, but they'd never forget him. "He's probably still dancin' a jig in heaven with his family!" Joe exclaimed. They smiled, remembering.

Memories of Thatcher Springs, the people that had grown closer than family, the love they shared, made Joe and Josh realize how homesick they really were. So much had happened since they arrived in Baker City. "It sure would be good to see 'em, Josh. We could bring Betsy and Sloan and Uncle Charlie too. Wouldn't Kate be surprised?" He looked over at his brother. "Don't give up, Josh. I pray for ya all the time, brother. I believe he's gonna heal ya."

Josh nodded his thanks, thinking about that scripture Eula Mae had left with him.

———

Sloan dashed up the stairs to the room she shared with Betsy, the letter hugged inside her coat. Betsy had gone to the ranch to work with Joe, deep cleaning and making repairs to the house. Josh, she noticed, was sleeping. She was grateful for the chance to read Alicia's letter in privacy, before the others knew about it. Her heart was racing with anticipation.

She opened it, breathing a prayer, not sure what to pray for. The first paragraph was characteristic of Alecia, chitchat before getting to the point.

> *We have been so very busy with several charities and piano recitals and preparing for the harsh winter that is expected. Of course Edward was instrumental in development of Providence Hospital, of which he will be head surgeon. The boys, Edward Jr. and William, are exceeding all expectations in their studies.*

At last she got to Britta.

> *Britta has applied for medical school, which you know, it is not easy for women to be accepted. She is confident and hopeful because of her experience assisting her*

*father for nearly the past five years. It's mainly because
of that that she will not be able to travel west. Were it
not for that opportunity, Sloan dear, I'm not sure it's
a good idea anyway. Do you truly think the "cousins"
should meet? At this point in their lives, I feel more
harm than good would come of it. Surely Betsy doesn't
know the facts.*

Sloan sat back in her chair, feeling the weight of disappointment.
The letter slipped to the floor. She felt sure Britta didn't have any
idea about the correspondence between her and Alecia. She was
second-guessing herself about having told Betsy the truth. *Oh Lord,
what have I done?*

Josh could read Sloan like a book. When she delivered his dinner
that night, it was obvious something was amiss. He didn't hesitate.
"Did the letter come today?"

She stared at him for a minute, then arranged his tray on the
bedside table. "Is it so obvious? Yes, a letter came today—from
Alecia. I'm quite sure Britta knows nothing of my invitation. Her
mother has made the decision for her. She won't be coming." Sloan
turned, heading back to the kitchen.

"Ma'am, I'd like to request some coffee. Two cups please. Maybe
it would help to talk about it. Come sit for a spell."

Sloan hesitated, then went to the kitchen, bringing back the
coffee. She sat on the edge of the rocking chair as if she didn't
intend to stay long. "I should have left it alone. Betsy has gone from
numbness to acceptance. Even to anticipation of seeing her sister.
Her twin sister! Now I will have to tell her Britta won't be coming."
She buried her head in her hands.

"Maybe not, Sloan. If it was the other way around, if Betsy was
invited out to New York, who would ya want to make that choice?
You? Or Betsy? How would you have handled it?"

Sloan was clearly deep in thought, considering the idea. "Well, I'm not exactly sure. I guess—no, I *know*—I would tell Betsy the truth. It's only right that it be her decision."

"And Britta has the right to make that choice too. Don't give up, Sloan. I promise whatever it takes will be worth it. I assure you it will be so worth it."

———

The following Sunday as the family gathered at McLemore Ranch, Sloan broke her silence, gathered her strength, and shared the letter. "Betsy and I, neither one wants to give up." She glanced at Josh. "I'm asking for your prayers and for advice. The issue of my daughters knowing one another has become vitally important to me. I accept responsibility for my choices in the past. I've always believed it best to leave well enough alone. But getting to know you two, Josh and Joe, has changed my thinking. Too many years have been lost." She blinked back threatening tears, unable to continue.

Uncle Charlie softened the tension. "Only thing I can think of sweeter than Betsy bein' here is two Betsys bein' here!" Everyone smiled. "Write again Sloan. Stay after it."

They held hands and prayed the same prayer Sloan had prayed all those years ago, in the bedroom of that very house. "Thy will be done, Lord. Thy will be done."

After more conversation, Jack, who had not spoken all evening, quietly raised his hand. Josh laughed. "This ain't school, buddy. What's on your mind?"

"I was trying to put myself in Britta's shoes. I know I'm only ten, but it seems to me that Betsy should be the one to write the letter. From Betsy straight to her sister."

———

The following Wednesday, Joe walked hand in hand with Betsy to post the letter. It was addressed to Miss Britta Lundgren, c/o Dr. Edward Lundgren, Providence Hospital, New York, New York.

She had felt strong and confident in the decision to write the letter herself. Had it not been for the wisdom of ten-year-old Jackson Witherspoon, it may never have occurred to her. The Witherspoons had raised a fine young man.

"What d'ya say we go to the coffee shop?" Joe smiled down at her, then quickly amended. "Not *that* one. The one across the street. Remember? The one you recommended the day we met?" She looped her arm through his as they walked that direction, both smiling. Betsy had never felt so happy.

Joe ordered. "Two coffees, please." He glanced behind the counter. "Does that happen to be huckleberry pie on the shelf?"

"Yes, sir. Brought in fresh this mornin by Mrs. McLemore herself! She's famous for it."

# Chapter 13

Since that day at the Home Cookin' Café, when the Reed brothers came in for supper, Betsy could hardly believe how everything had changed. Her young life had been a story of blisters and callouses, of loneliness. Cowboys passing through would flirt with the petite blonde waitress from time to time. And the Jones boy at church wanted to court her; at least it was rumored. In secret, Betsy didn't see a future for herself in Baker City. But she would never leave Sloan. Sloan McLemore was not only her mother, but her best and dearest friend.

So much had happened. The news that she had a twin sister seemed like a dream: overwhelming on one hand, thrilling on the other. Even now she'd had to pinch herself. *I have a sister!* She prayed Britta would write to say she was coming to Oregon.

The fact that the mortgage on McLemore Ranch had been paid off, that the continuous struggle to make payments had come to an end, was a huge answer to prayer. The weight of it had felt endless: mother and daughter working their fingers to the bone. And now their ranch was "free and clear."

But overriding these miracles, the thing that played again and again in her mind was that Joe had said he loved her. Handsome, hardworking, caring, wonderful Joseph Reed loved her. *I always believed, Lord, that you heard my prayers, that you would answer. I always believed. But now that your hand is evident on my life, I can hardly believe it! Thank you, Lord, thank you from my heart.*

———

All Joe could think about was proposing to Betsy. He wanted her for his wife. He would need to speak with Sloan of course but realized timing wasn't the best, with the turmoil over Britta. Then there was Josh. He was guilt-ridden to feel such happiness when his twin brother lay paralyzed, not knowing if he'd ever walk again. They had done everything together. Would Joe's marriage to Betsy bring separation between them? He decided to speak with Josh first, maybe even ask his advice about talking to Sloan. *Lord, I need wisdom. Please help me.*

Joe and Betsy had lingered over their coffee long after the pie was gone. Betsy broke into his thoughts. "I better get back, Joey. We're scheduled to clean the church buildin' today, me and Mama."

"Why don't I help you clean it? Give Sloan a break."

"You sure you can handle a feather duster?" Betsy teased, laughing her adorable laugh—the one with the dimple.

"Well, who do ya think yer talkin' to? Kate had us boys cleanin' house once a week. In fact, you and me, we make a good pair. I can clean and you can shoot." He winked.

That really got her laughing. She slapped him on the arm. "That's what I love about you, Joe." Her smiling face turned serious as they looked in each other's eyes. She hadn't ever said out loud that she loved him. She looked down into her empty cup, and then up at him with big, blue eyes. "I do, Joey. I love you."

Joe forgot about the plans he'd just made in his mind. "Betsy," he reached for her hand. "Sweet Betsy." He shook his head in wonder, his eyes glistening. "Will you marry me?"

———

The church building was cold as a cave. Joe got a fire going in the wood stove and brought in several armloads to fill the wood box. Betsy came up next to him with the broom and feather duster. "Take your pick!" Betsy exclaimed, her face beaming. Neither had been able to stop smiling since she had said *yes*.

"I pick you!" Joe exclaimed and pulled her to him, the broom and duster falling to the floor as she wrapped her arms around his neck. He kissed her gently, and then deeply, with longing. Betsy didn't hold back—until a deep voice came from somewhere behind them. "Ahem." The pastor had walked in. Betsy was mortified. Joe didn't skip a beat. He quickly pulled off his hat. "We were hoping you'd be here, sir. Betsy and me, well, she said yes, and well, guess we need ta plan a weddin'!"

That night, after everyone had turned in, Joe drug his bedroll into Josh's room. "We havin' a campout?" Josh laughed.

"Why not, brother? Haven't spent much time together lately." Joe hadn't stopped smiling since he came through the door. He spread out the bedroll then headed back toward the kitchen. "I'll see what I can find for a midnight snack."

Joe brought in a tray with cinnamon rolls and milk and settled in the rocking chair, happiness filling him from head to toe.

Josh chuckled. "So when's the weddin'?"

"What are ya talkin' about?" Joe said, his mouth full. "Is it that obvious?"

"Just a lucky guess. Besides, as Max would say, I can read ya like a book."

The room was quiet, as the brothers simultaneously dunked their sticky rolls in cool milk, enjoying every slurpy bite. After a bit, Joe grew thoughtful. "You know I'm crazy over Betsy. We wanta get married, Josh. She actually said *yes*. I just wanta be sure—"

Josh cut him off. "Joe, I know what you're thinkin'. You're worried that it's somehow not right because of—me. But what if it was the other way around? Wouldn't ya want me ta be happy?"

"I *do* want you to be happy, Josh. I'd give up my own happiness for you, brother."

"And I'd give up mine for you, Joey."

## Part 2

# BRITTA LUNDGREN

*"For I know the plans I have for you," declares the Lord; "plans to prosper you and not to harm you, plans to give you hope and a future."*
—*Jeremiah 29:11*

# Chapter 14

Britta was thrilled with the inauguration of New York's Providence Hospital—with its modern capabilities, large wards, and gleaming floors. She would be working there in the same capacity, under her father's direction, as his assistant. Her lifelong dream was to be a doctor herself, to have a degree in medicine, to have her own practice. Ever since Britta was old enough to read, she had poured through her father's medical journals with keen interest on all the latest developments in medicine.

Britta Lundgren was not only smart; she was also beautiful. She could have her pick of fine young men, those of high station and social status, handsome, sophisticated, from families of wealth. Her own family was very rich and lived in one of New York's finest manors. It was truly a showplace with sprawling manicured grounds and a circular drive featuring a magnificent fountain. Edward and Alecia Lundgren were known for hosting gala affairs in their home, unique, in that the third floor was a ballroom.

Each morning when she arrived at the hospital, Britta would check her box for the letter of acceptance from medical school. She had completed the application process, passed preliminary testing, and met every qualification. Even though it remained a long shot for women to be accepted, Britta was certain she would be—because of her father, if for no other reason. She could hardly wait.

Carter, one of the Lundgren house servants, drove Britta to the hospital by horse and buggy early each morning. That particular morning, the surrounding area seemed more congested than usual as he pulled to a stop in front of the hospital entrance. Inside was even more so. During the night, there had been rioting in Lower Manhattan, causing an influx of wounded as if from a war zone. In another wing, a mission group had rounded up ailing, homeless children from the streets of Brooklyn and transported them to Providence. For the first time since the opening, every room was full, with an overflow of patients lining the halls.

Britta found her father coming out of the surgical area to ask how she could best help. "You are most needed in the children's wing, my dear. I am on my way there shortly to begin examinations. I would like you to carefully clean each child as best you can. And Britta, be watchful of head lice."

As she entered the closed double doors to the children's wing of the hospital, it seemed deathly quiet for a unit filled with children. Each ward held eight beds, occupied with small forms, and cots along the hallway were full with the overflow. Soft crying and whimpering could be heard; the smell of impoverished conditions permeated the place.

Dr. Lundgren had cautioned his daughter, early on, about becoming emotionally involved with their patients. Over several years of assisting him in his small New York clinic, she had developed a rather hard veneer emulating the good doctor, being very careful to treat the wounded and monitor the sick without getting attached to the patient. But with little ones, it was different. After the first few hours, her heart was breaking for those sick, impoverished children.

She was tending a little Chinese girl, gently washing her limp body with warm soapy water. The little girl was about four, Britta guessed, and seemed in a coma. Even so, Britta subconsciously began to quietly sing to her. Suddenly, dark almond eyes popped open pleadingly. "Sissy?" she barely uttered the question.

"What is your name, little one?" Britta asked. The child reminded her of the china doll in her doll collection: delicate features.

Again, the child asked, "My Sissy?" Tears pooled in her sad eyes.

"Did your sister come here? To the hospital with you?"

"Yes. She is sick. Please find her?"

"What about your mother and father?" Britta feared the answer.

"They went to heaven."

Britta stroked the girl's hair and again asked, "What is your name, dear?"

"Liu." And then the child lapsed back to unconsciousness.

Britta continued her rounds, hoping to find Liu's sister. One of the ladies from the Mission Society was sitting at the bedside of a young Italian girl. While Britta attended the child, she and the women quietly chatted. "Do you recall bringing in two Chinese girls? Sisters?" Britta inquired hopefully.

"Hmm. No, I don't, but I've mainly been working in Little Italy. I will ask some of the others."

Britta checked back on Liu before she left for the day. "Did you find her?" the little girl asked weakly.

"Not yet, darling, but the hospital is very crowded. She must be here somewhere." She took the girl's little hand in hers. "Others are looking for her too." Britta tried to sound confident. "Good people." A thought struck her. "I will come first thing in the morning, Liu, and bring a gift—just for you!" Perhaps a thread of hope would keep the little girl alive. She was so pale and limp.

It was Britta's father who told her that Liu's sister had died of typhoid fever. She was eleven. The two had been found living in squalor, orphaned and near starvation. It broke Britta's heart. *Lord, I don't understand how this can be. Please forgive me, but I cannot tell Liu the truth.*

It was barely dawn the next morning when Britta asked Carter to drive her to the hospital. She hurried through the big double doors, carrying a bundle wrapped in pink tissue paper—her gift to little Liu. When she entered the ward, everything looked as it had yesterday, the beds filled with sleeping children. Except there against the back wall, Liu's bed sat empty. It was made up with clean white sheets; all traces of the child were gone.

Hours had passed when Dr. Lundgren found his daughter curled up on the stark white bed, clutching a soft toy lamb to her breast. She stared at the wall, dried tears stained her face. "Britta?" her father called in alarm. "Britta. Are you all right?"

At dinner that night, Britta had no appetite. It was all she could do to sit there in the opulence of their dining room. The fine china, crystal, polished silver, and the table spread with an abundance of decadent foods, seemed to her a crime, in light of starving children. She wanted to excuse herself.

Alecia broke into her thoughts. "Britta dear, the dressmaker will be here in the morning to go over your fabric selection for a new ball gown." She noticed her daughter not eating, merely shoving the food around on her plate. "Hilly left samples in your room." She smiled brightly. "I would love to see you in red velvet for the holidays this year."

Edward Jr. and William looked at each other with matching smirks. "Ha! That'll be the day—when she picks red!" William exclaimed.

"Sit up and eat your vegetables, boys." Today had been tough on the doctor too.

When Britta finally did escape to her room, all she wanted was to climb into bed. But of course, faithful Hilly knocked softly and came in to attend her. Without speaking, she carefully helped Britta out of her dress and into her nightgown, motioned to the dressing table where Hilly gently unclipped her hair, and began the nightly routine of brushing her silky locks. "Wash your face now, baby. I'll bring up a cup of cocoa. It'll help you sleep."

Britta loved Hilda Durant. The sturdy woman had brought her into the world and been her nurse and her nanny. They had shared their hopes and dreams. They had prayed together and laughed together. Sometimes cried together. Neither thought twice about the fact that twenty years were between them. That one was mistress and one servant. That Britta was white and Hilly a black woman. They were best friends. When Hilda returned with the cocoa, she announced, "Tomorrow, baby, we're going upstate for a few days. I spoke with you father. He thinks it's a fine idea." Hilly noticed the fabric swatches undisturbed. "I'm assuming it's the deep blue velvet?" Britta loved the color blue.

When at last Britta did sink into her feather bed, hot tears came once more, for the tiny Chinese girl, Liu. *All she wanted was her sister, Lord. I pray they are together now.*

# Chapter 15

It had been a fine idea indeed to get out of the city, to visit her grandparents in upstate New York. Their estate was a breathtaking sight this time of year; the colors of fall lined the long drive, and red and gold leaves swirling about on the wind. The house and horse barns rose into sight, as they came over the hill, stark white as if freshly painted. Britta was feeling better already with new appreciation for the peacefulness of the place, the fresh air. The anticipation of riding one of her grandparents' horses began to revive her.

The Lundgrens, Edward's parents, were well known for their fine highbred jumpers, mostly Thoroughbreds because of their athletic conformation and stamina. Their farm trained upward of thirty horses at a time, with world-renowned trainers onsite. Britta's grandparents had retired to a degree but stayed on top of every aspect of the farm – breeding, training, sales, and overseeing the trainers and maintenance crew. House servants were treated more like family and though their home boasted an elaborate dining room, they all sat in the kitchen together for dinner. An outsider would probably not know who were the owners and who were the workers. Britta loved that about her grandparents; her grandmother rarely wore anything but jodhpurs and tall riding boots.

Britta appreciated the challenge of jumping, but mostly she loved the freedom of riding. The land beyond the training area, covered miles of gently rolling fields. There was something about the abandon she felt, riding alone, her hair loosened from the usual ivory combs, the wind in her face. Of the horses she was given to choose from, Lancelot was her pick. He was glossy black and seemed to thrive in the same freedom: horse and rider one. When she returned to the stables late afternoon, Britta felt refreshed. She insisted on brushing down Sir Lancelot herself, although two groomers met her at the gate.

The house was filled with delicious aromas coming from the kitchen. Even though the domestic help included two cooks, Mrs. Lundgren loved to pitch in with the cooking. "Gram! Do I smell potato pancakes?" Britta was hungry for the first time in a week.

"Yes, darling. Just for you, my beautiful granddaughter! Of course, Grandfather insisted on roast beef and all the trimmings. And Sally has made a special dessert for us to enjoy in the parlor, after supper."

Later that night as Hilly was brushing out Britta's hair, she commented, "Baby, you seem like a different person out here. Is it the air? The horse ridin'? Maybe the food? Or could it be just gettin' away from doctorin'?" Britta was quiet.

"I think," she began at last, "it's all of that. About the air and riding and Gram's wonderful food. And that she likes to eat in the kitchen with the help. And that she cooks right along with them. I've never known my grandparents to put on fancy clothes and go to a ball. Even though they are no doubt wealthier than the crowd my parents hob nob with, they don't really care to be part of high society."

"And the doctorin'?" Hilly pressed on.

"I want to be a doctor, Hilly, you know that as much as anybody. Nothing has changed." Britta realized she hadn't checked her mailbox since before—Liu. She'd forgotten about the letter from medical school. Maybe it would be there when they returned. "I don't know. It's so rewarding just to see ailing people well again; broken bones mend; fevers break." She was quiet once more. Hilly waited, slowly brushing her long golden tresses. "But when a child dies—" She couldn't continue.

Hilly was thoughtful. "You're an exceptional young woman, Britta. God has a plan for ya, baby. He knows the plans he's got for you."

———

The trip back home offered Britta little time to make the transition from her carefree days at her grandparents, back to work in the hospital and back to her "social calendar." Alecia expected her to attend the women's gatherings, especially the monthly tea and poetry readings, rubbing shoulders with New York's elite women. And of course, she would be required to attend, as well as take part in the planning of, her parents' annual Holiday Ball. It was presumed Britta would help with the menu decisions and decorating plans. She would be scheduled for fittings of her ball gown. The whole extravaganza would be another occasion where Alecia concocted tactics for Britta to dance with certain eligible bachelors. Britta knew her mother only meant well. But how she dreaded it.

The hospital was busy, but not the chaos as before. The children were mostly gone, some well enough to be taken to Brooklyn's orphanage, which was a step better than the streets they had come from. Some remained, still battling disease and malnutrition. Some like Liu didn't make it. Britta kept her focus on the business at hand, caring for the aging, avoiding the children's wing.

At last she finished her shift and hurried to retrieve the mail before Carter arrived with the buggy. The box was full, after a week's time, so she stuffed its contents into her bag and dashed out front. She would go through it at home.

Dinner was served promptly at seven each evening in the Lundgren dining room. Edward was often late since the hospital had opened, but Alecia expected the rest of the family to be there on time. The boys were in their chairs anxiously waiting, delicious smells from the kitchen tantalizing their senses, when Alecia joined them. She rang the silver bell. The staff began serving the meal; silver platters beautifully displayed on burgundy linen offered a bounty of roasted chicken, boiled potatoes, milk gravy, baked squash, and greens. To top it off, Rosa delivered a plate of hot biscuits, butter, and honey. "Where is Britta?" Alecia asked no one in particular. "Rosa, please have Hilly check on Britta. Perhaps she fell asleep."

The door was locked. "Britta honey, is everything alright?" Hilly had never been locked out. "Are ya sick, baby?"

"I need to be alone, Hilly. Tell Mother I won't be down for dinner." Britta's voice sounded strange, cold—not herself.

Hilly turned to go, her brow furrowed with worry. "I'll bring up a cup of cocoa."

"No." Britta answered abruptly. "No, thank you. I'm already in bed."

The letter was still clutched in Britta's hand as she lay curled in bed, too dazed to cry, too stunned to pray. *How could they not tell me? Seventeen years! How could they do this to me!* She had read and reread a dozen times the unbelievable words "we are sisters."

Revelations kept coming. *My parents are not my parents, my brothers* — "Oh God. What is happening? Who am I?" She had never gotten past the letter from Oregon—from Betsy McLemore, *her twin sister.* The rest of the mail lay on the floor, unopened.

Hilly returned later, knocking softly. There was no answer. Alecia tried a bit later. "Britta? Britta are you ill? Please unlock the door dear." Still no answer.

By the time her father came home, Alecia and Hilly were consumed with worry. Their best guess was that Britta had not been accepted to medical school. Edward approached his daughter's room and rapped softly. "Britta darling, can we talk?" He waited. "If this is about medical school, there are others, sweetheart." It was quiet as a tomb. He was thinking of a different approach when the door latch sounded and the door opened slowly. Britta was walking away, toward the rocking chair by her bed. Hilly had rocked her in that same chair as a baby. She sat now, holding out the envelope to her father.

To his alarm the letter was not from medical school. He could perhaps have offered a resolution, had that been the case. He sat on the edge of the bed, staring at the letter in his hand, from Oregon. Dread filled him as he struggled to say something.

Britta spoke first, her voice cold and calculated. "Go ahead. Read it." Her father hesitated. "Just read it, Father." Slowly, Edward pulled the letter from its envelope, carefully unfolding the pages.

*Dear Britta,*

*I pray to God: please guide my words. You have been known to me as my cousin who lives in New York, that not only distance separates us but status as well. We are worlds apart. But it's only right that I share with you something I've just learned myself. I know this truth will be difficult for you as it was for me—in the beginning.*

*Mama was a very young woman, just one year older than me, when her husband—my father—was murdered. They were expecting their first child. I can't even imagine how difficult it was for her. She wrote to her sister, your mother, Aunt Alecia, asking her to consider adopting the baby.*

*Oh Britta, I hope and pray you will receive this news with understanding. Two babies were born. You and me. We are not cousins but sisters. We are sisters, Britta. Twins.*

*We have been deprived of seventeen years of growing up together, seventeen years of heartbreak for Mama. At first I was so distressed and hurt. I cried for days and prayed. God has revealed to me the true blessing of it. I pray you will consider traveling to Oregon. I so want to know you, to make up for lost time. I confess it took a while to grasp it all. But now, I can only think about knowing my sister.*

*Yours truly,*
*Betsy*

Edward was speechless. His handsome face seemed to age before Britta's eyes. He raked a hand through his graying hair. Without looking up, he simply said, "We thought it was best. Best for you, for Betsy—for your mother."

"Which mother?" she snapped.

He looked up at her, recognizing for the first time she was still in yesterday's clothes, her hair tangled, dark circles beneath her eyes. "Britta." He choked back tears. "I love you like you were my own flesh and blood. I held you the day you were born. Your—mother— and I, we truly believed we were doing the right thing." He shook his head, looking down at the letter still in his hand. "I'm sorry you had to find out this way."

With her jaw clenched, she spat out, "Well, at least my *sister* had the courage to tell me!" And then she burst into long-held tears, sobbing her heart out. Her father went to her and wrapped her in his arms. She didn't resist but collapsed against his chest.

Britta stayed in her room all day. She didn't change her clothes or comb her hair, refused food, wouldn't see anyone. Late afternoon she heard noises outside the bedroom door, furniture scraping the hardwood floors. After several minutes had passed, Britta heard a voice from the other side of the door. Hilly's voice. "Guess I'll just go ahead and have this here tea party by myself." When Britta was a little girl she and Hilly had secret tea parties in her bedroom.

Britta couldn't help but smile. She tiptoed over and peeked through the keyhole. There sat Hilly in a chair, holding a big tray on her lap. Slowly Britta opened the door. As if she was still seven, Hilly bustled in, set the tray on the floor, and gathered two bed pillows for them to sit on. She poured hot tea from the blue china teapot Britta loved and broke open a scone for each, buttered them, and spooned drippy berry jam inside. Neither spoke.

After a bit, Hilly looked up. "Want seconds, baby?"

They talked and cried some, Hilly telling how all those years ago, both women had prayed all night. "Sloan never expected to find a baby that morning when the rest of us rode out—with you. She believed it was God's will that Lundgrens take both babies. Alecia believed it was God's will that Sloan keep one. You became Edward and Alecia's child more and more with each mile of that long train ride back to New York. They are wonderful parents to you, child. You have a blessed life."

That night, Britta went down to dinner. Everyone spoke cordially, though tension was in the air. At least it was, until Edward Jr. took a big bite of mashed potatoes, only to discover they'd been laced with horseradish. He jumped up fanning his face, knocking over the water goblet as he desperately reached for it. Their father, already tense from the events of the day, jumped up, knocking the Queen Anne chair from beneath him. Alecia was ringing the silver bell furiously. "Hilly? Rosa!" Little William remained calm, enjoying the whole scene.

Britta was not about to let her mischievous little brother get away with it. She carefully placed a pea in the tip of her spoon and pinged him right between the eyes. Of course, that invited a pea fight, which no one seemed to notice since it took all the adults present to put out the fire in poor Edward Jr.'s mouth.

# Chapter 16

Alecia and Britta met in the parlor after everyone had gone to bed. They wore their robes. Hilly brought in steaming hot cocoa, stoked the fire, and bid them good-night. The tension between mother and daughter slowly eased; there was something about seeing her mother with her hair down and in her nightclothes. It had been Alecia's idea that they talk.

"It was an answer to prayer." Alecia began slowly, "We didn't think we were able to have children. I could not conceive in those early years." She bit her lip, as emotion threatened. Britta sat quietly, waiting for her mother to continue. "Your father and I prayed fervently for a child. For six years we prayed. When the letter came from Sloan"— She couldn't finish. They sipped their cocoa silently.

"You were both so tiny. Edward thought since you seemed the strongest, we should choose you. It could easily have been the other way around. It was a shock to Sloan, to everyone, that two babies were born. Hilly was an experienced midwife, but she had never delivered twins." Britta could barely breathe. She knew this was difficult for her mother. She felt compassion for her but still could not speak, could not move.

"I prayed all night that God's will be done. Sloan confessed in a letter that she had prayed the same and that God had surely answered. Betsy was her salvation. We both believed we did the right thing. We truly believed." Alecia was crying now and Britta couldn't hold back her own tears any longer.

It seemed they sat crying silent tears for a long time, both struggling to grasp the weight of it all. Finally, Britta moved to the settee where her mother sat, legs curled up beneath her. Mother and daughter embraced. Through her tears, Britta said, "I love you, Mother."

———

The next morning, after a night of praying and fitful sleep, Britta slipped out of bed before dawn. On one hand, she felt drained like a rag doll. But on the other, a new objective was beginning to take shape in her mind. She lit the lamps and stirred the remains of last night's fire, bringing it back to life, adding a small log. Then she straightened her room, hung up clothes that had been tossed about, and smoothed her bed. Britta gathered the mail, still scattered on the floor, and wrapped herself in a blanket as she settled in the rocking chair. There it was. The letter from medical school. Somehow, it had lost significance in light of the other letter. The one from her sister Betsy. "I have a sister," she said aloud to the empty room.

She would have been terribly upset, had she opened the medical school's letter first. With the plans swirling in her mind, perhaps it was the best-case scenario. Britta Lundgren had been, in fact, accepted to medical school. However, for women students, a prerequisite study was required. The next opportunity for her admittance to that class was September of the following year. Britta could not begin school for eleven months. "Nearly a year!" she exclaimed. *Lord, you surely do work in mysterious ways.*

At the hospital later that morning, Britta checked in with her father to discuss her duties for the day. "And Father, would there be a chance we could have lunch together? Maybe in your office?"

Dr. Lundgren had a full schedule, but he knew his daughter had something on her mind. "Of course, sweetheart. Why don't you bring a tray—just before noon?"

---

Edward waited until he and his wife were alone in their bedchambers that night, to speak of Britta's plans. Alecia was brushing her hair at the dressing table. He sat on the edge of the bed. "She wants to go to Oregon," he said flatly.

Alecia stopped brushing and looked at her husband's reflection in the mirror. "Well, of course. Someday, perhaps it will work out to take a family trip to Oregon. We are much too busy for that now, dear."

He looked at his wife's face in the mirror. She was still beautiful. Britta resembled her in many ways. "She's intending to go after Christmas." Edward felt drained.

From her bedroom down the hall, Britta could hear her parents arguing and knew it was about her. She hated to be the cause of turmoil in their lives. But had they not created havoc in hers? Hilly was a comforting sight when she knocked at the door a bit later. Instead of the nightly routine, Britta invited her to sit in the rocker. "I've been feeling so scattered, Hilly, like my world was being torn apart. I thought my future was mapped out, secure." Britta had been pacing as she spoke. She plopped down on the dressing table chair, turning to face her friend. "Last night I prayed. Really prayed. I haven't talked to God like that in a long time."

"And?" Hilly urged her on, listening intently.

"I don't know if it was God telling me or *me* telling me. But when I woke up this morning, I knew I had to go to Oregon. I have to meet the rest of my family. Betsy. I must know her." She took a shaky breath. "I'm going, Hilly, and I want you to come with me."

---

Thanksgiving had been delightful. Britta's grandparents came to the city and stayed for a week. The three women went Christmas shopping and trimmed the house with greens, red velvet ribbons, and candles. Grandfather took the boys out to select a Christmas tree that would be delivered and set up in the parlor, the fragrance of it filling the house. Britta loved this time of year: the shopping, the decorating, her brothers playing Christmas carols on the piano—or at least giving it their best. It seemed she had a new appreciation for the goings-on, and for her family. She saw the social events, a dread in the past, in a new light. *Maybe because I'm leaving soon,* she thought. Even the Holiday Ball, only a week away, did not fill her with the usual trepidation.

Hilly was skilled at turning Britta's blonde locks into a stunning upsweep of curls, leaving tendrils around her face. She carefully placed pearl hairpins that would match her pearl choker, a Christmas gift from her mother. The royal blue velvet gown had turned out picture-perfect. With a fitted bodice that complemented Britta's tiny waist and the deep blue against her flawless skin, it had been the ideal choice. Alecia had selected the pattern, off the shoulders and the jewelry: pearls accented with sapphire gems. When she was all put together, Hilly stepped back, shaking her head. "I declare! Ya look like royalty, baby. Like the queen of New York City!"

To Alecia's way of thinking, the trip to Oregon was a passing fancy. Britta would get over it, especially if some young man swept her off her feet at the ball. She had made sure the cream of New York's crop would be in attendance. Alecia was quite the charming hostess, as always, but kept her eye on Britta the whole evening, watching her swirl around the dance floor with at least a dozen handsome young men, truly the belle of the ball.

One of those eligible bachelors had come calling just before Christmas Day, delivering a gift from his family, a thank-you present for the lovely party. Alecia invited him into the parlor for a cup of cider and went immediately to find Britta. "Patrick O'Conner is in the parlor, dear. He asked to see you." Alecia was certain that was the reason for his visit, even though he hadn't actually said it.

"Oh?" Britta looked puzzled. "I don't recall a Patrick O'Conner."

"Well, please join us for a few minutes. His family sent a thank-you gift." Alecia looked her daughter over, tucking an unruly strand of hair behind her ear and straightening the sash at her waist. "Come along, Britta darling."

After Patrick presented the gift, a lovely silver candlestick, he said, "I've also come to invite the Lundgren family to our home for a New Year celebration, a week from Sunday." He smiled proudly and said, "It will be a traditional Irish feast."

"How lovely!" Alecia exclaimed, clasping her hands together. "The Lundgren family gratefully accepts your kind invitation." She was all smiles.

Patrick shyly directed his attention toward Britta. "And if I'm not being too presumptuous, Miss Lundgren, may I escort you to the celebration?"

"Thank you, sir. I do appreciate your bidding, but I'm afraid I can't accept." Britta smiled brightly. Her mother blanched. "I'll be on the train to Oregon."

---

Even as Alecia helped her daughter pack, she couldn't believe it was really happening. She was sure Britta would change her mind, especially with all the reasons she suggested to postpone the trip. "The weather couldn't be worse for travel, Britta. You very likely could be detained for—who knows how long? In some wretched train station."

"I appreciate your concern, Mother, but the tickets have been purchased and I'm nearly packed. Bedsides, Hilly will be with me and Father has arranged for the best accommodations money can buy. I'll be fine." Britta really wished her mother would leave her be.

With the sound of breaking glass, Britta got her wish. Alecia hurried to the top of the stairs, shouting at her rambunctious boys.

In spite of the drama of their departure, Britta and Hilly finally boarded the train bound for Chicago, the first leg of a very long trip to Oregon.

# Chapter 17

It was a cold snowy morning in Baker City as Betsy and Sloan dressed for church. They were staying in town this Sunday; Uncle Charlie and Joe would ride in from McLemore Ranch, driving the buckboard. Charlie had a saddle to deliver, and of course, after a week away, Joe was busting at the seams to see Betsy.

"I must say the dress turned out near perfect, Betsy. That deep blue cotton makes your eyes look extra blue. And your hair looks pretty too, pulled back like that." Sloan was happy and grateful to see her daughter, suddenly a beautiful young woman. She laughed. "Ya look like a queen! The queen of Baker City." Betsy felt like a queen in her new dress, new boots, and wool cape given her by Eula Mae. It was a soft dark-blue wool with a hood and a little fur trim. Betsy had never owned anything so special.

Sloan looked lovely too in a suit also given by Eula Mae. She had altered it to fit her perfectly. The deep forest green, she admitted to herself, made her feel like a queen too. In fact, Sloan looked younger these days, the worry lines replaced by her lovely smile. She had more energy, more—hope. It wasn't the new clothes, or even that the mortgage on the ranch had been paid off. Those were huge blessings, no doubt about it. What truly changed her countenance was a new freedom. She still worked just as hard at the boardinghouse, and so did Betsy. But having confessed the secret she'd held for seventeen years, releasing the hold it had on her, seemed to take years off her life. Today, though nervous about it, she would stand before the congregation and tell them about Britta.

Josh had been getting around quite well in his fancy wheelchair. Along with his right-hand man, Jack, they could get the thing almost anywhere. Although he longed to be horseback, the wheelchair had given Josh new freedom, not to mention a hard workout. His upper body had strengthened considerably and the fresh cold air had given him the healthy look of a cowboy. Except that he couldn't walk, Josh and Joe looked exactly alike again. This Sunday morning, he and Jack would take the shortcut to church, grinding through crunchy fresh snow.

Now that winter set in, the carpenter, Hans Steffen, could get to work on Mrs. Witherspoon's home, replacing the damaged walls of her kitchen. Hans and his crew had been under a deadline to finish the exterior of Dr. Cartwright's new hospital. The town had well outgrown the one-bed facility behind his office, the room where Josh had spent his first few weeks after being shot in the back. The new Baker Hospital would have four rooms on each of two floors, along with additional space for doc's office and a surgical room. The townsfolk watched the progress with great anticipation. The hospital would be the biggest building ever to go up in Baker City.

After the usual three hymns, a prayer, and communion, the preacher at last introduced Sloan. The congregation sat straighter, some glancing at each other, wondering what Sloan McLemore had to share. She smiled, nodded a greeting to the crowd, and began. "Thank you, all—each of you for the love you've shown me and Betsy over the years." Sloan paused, willing herself not to cry, and then continued the story that began so long ago. Before she got to the part about there being two babies, Betsy stood and went to her mother's side, putting her arm around Sloan's waist, giving support.

Sloan swallowed hard and took a deep breath. She looked out at Uncle Charlie who was nodding as if to say everything would be all right. In fact, the whole congregation looked at her with love. Sloan had been a true servant to all, nursing the sick, teaching the children, cleaning the building, and preparing food for special occasions and those in need. Then she looked at Josh and Joe. Twins. Handsome, strong, their two sets of deep brown eyes imploring her to continue. She took strength from them and went ahead. "Two baby girls were born that day. Betsy is a twin. Her sister was adopted by Alecia and Edward Lundgren, my sister and brother-in-law." Sloan put her arm around Betsy's shoulder, pulling her closer. "I'm sorry to have kept this secret from Betsy, and from all of you. You are like our family. I'm so sorry." She could no longer hold back the tears. Mother and daughter embraced as the people of Baker City Baptist Church sat stunned. Suddenly, Jackson Witherspoon stood and began clapping! All the others began clapping too until the whole congregation stood. "We love ya, Sloan! We love ya, Betsy!" They shouted out their support until Betsy faced them, with her own words.

"Britta, my sister, left New York last week. That's where she grew up, in New York City." Betsy had a huge smile on her face as she made this declaration. "And she's coming here, to Baker! She'll be here in a few weeks!" She couldn't help but laugh with excitement. "Just so y'all don't think yer seein' double when she gets here!" She looked at Joe. The big strong cowboy, with eyes pooling, blew her a kiss.

———

Once settled in their private Pullman car, their trunks stored, Britta and Hilly began to relax and take in the luxurious appointments of their accommodations. A low whistle escaped Hilly. "Lands a Goshen! Doc Lundgren didn't spare no change on this fancy car." Her eyes were huge, taking in the leather lounge chairs and polished mahogany panels. The arched ceiling was painted with a peaceful mural, complemented by crystal chandeliers that sent shafts of light like twinkling stars throughout the chamber. The curtains were of the finest brocade, a European feel. Mirrors in gilded frames were fixed between the windows. Hilly, although a free black woman, would not have been allowed in that compartment, had she not been traveling as Britta's servant.

Britta sat on one of the velvet chairs next to the carved dining table. "Listen to this!" she exclaimed, picking up the evening menu. "What sounds good, Hilly? Roasted pheasant? Beefsteak? Or how about Maine lobster?" The two laughed all evening as the porter rapped on the door with each course. When he brought dessert, he quietly prepared their two beds, leaving a chocolate on their pillows.

The next morning, they made their way to the observation car, just to see what it was like. Britta loved watching the sights go by; even the bleak winter landscape seemed beautiful to her, peaceful. There was no pressure of social events, and even though she missed working at the hospital, she enjoyed the freedom in doing nothing. Of course, she had brought reading material: medical books and journals.

Their loyal porter found them, to take refreshment orders. "I will deliver your tray right away, Miss Lundgren."

Sitting across from them, a dapper older gentleman nodded and politely asked, "Excuse me. Are you by chance Dr. Lundgren's daughter? From New York?"

"Why yes, I am," Britta answered cautiously.

"Please allow me to introduce myself. My name is Thomas Crane. Your father and I are friends and business associates. I very much admire Dr. Lundgren."

"How nice to make your acquaintance, sir. And please meet my—dear friend, Hilda Durant." Britta was not about to say Hilly was her maid.

They discovered that Mr. Crane was also bound for Oregon. "Please feel free to send your porter after me, should you ladies need assistance during the trip."

Shortly after Britta and Hilly enjoyed their crunchy scones and hot tea, they returned to their private quarters. "Mr. Crane seems very nice. It's comforting to know we can call on him if necessary," Britta said as she removed her hat, plopped down, and put her feet up on the lounge. Hilly agreed. What they didn't know, when Britta's father had discovered that Thomas Crane, a private detective, was traveling west on an assignment, Dr. Lundgren paid him to keep an eye on his daughter. After all, despite her independent spirit, Britta was only seventeen.

As the train chugged on, both women relaxed more with each mile. They walked from one car to another to stretch their legs and nearly every day spent an hour or two in the observation car. The farther west they traveled, the more the landscape changed. In Wyoming, a tribe of friendly Indians rode their painted ponies alongside the tracks, racing the train, laughing, and waving at passengers. Another day it was a herd of buffalo churning a cloud of dust as they thundered along parallel to the mighty Transcontinental.

One evening as they were about to retire, suddenly the train came to a screeching halt. The abrupt stop caused the chandeliers to swing wildly and sent their books and other belongings flying. Hilly was already in her nightclothes and had just finished plating Britta's hair into a long, thick braid that hung down her back. She was still dressed. "I'll go see what happened, Hilly." She raced out the door.

The folks in the next car were just as perplexed, leaning against the windows trying to see up ahead. Everyone was talking at once, conjecturing perhaps, a boulder had fallen on the tracks. It was not only dusk, but foggy, making for poor visibility.

Britta continued toward the next car. Just as she pushed through the door, a rough arm yanked her back, the cold barrel of a gun jammed against her neck. She swallowed a scream. Something told her to submit, not to fight whoever had her. Straight ahead, facing her from the other end of the car, another bandit held a rifle on the passengers, his hat pulled down, a bandana tied over his mouth and nose.

"Good timing, little lady." The man gripped her long braid and with the pistol still in hand removed his grimy cowboy hat and shoved it at her midsection. "You're gonna help us out here."

He pressed the gun back to the side of her neck, right below her ear, still holding tight to her braid, and ordered her to start walking down the aisle, collecting valuables from the passengers: jewelry, watches, cash. "You jest fill up that hat little lady, and nobody gets hurt."

Britta complied, nodding to each passenger as they handed over their valuables, hoping to convey a confidence she didn't quite feel. She prayed someone would come to their rescue. It reminded her somehow of setting a broken bone. You just did it, and took a breath later. When they were halfway through the car, the other train robber backed out as if needed elsewhere. At least the odds were better. If only Mr. Crane were here.

It happened so fast. A voice came from somewhere behind. "Let her go, cowboy. Now!" It was Hilly! The bandit whirled, shoving Britta across the laps of an elderly couple. A shot rang out. The outlaw yelped, stumbled, and then collapsed to the floor.

Britta scrambled to her feet crying out to Hilly, who just stood there, holding a pistol, looking down at the victim lying on the floor. Just then Mr. Crane stepped up behind Britta, a gun in his hand. "I didn't kill him, Miss Lundgren, just stopped him. The other two are tied up in the next car. It's the Brumleys. The Brumley brothers from Texas are notorious train robbers," he stated with authority. "But not this time. Not on my watch."

When the bad guys were secured in a guarded prison car and valuables given back to their rightful owners, the train lurched to a start. Britta and Hilly gratefully returned to the privacy of their Pullman car. Hilly quickly tossed the pistol on the bed, like it was a hot potato, and wiped the perspiration from her brow. Britta was still in a daze. "I had no idea you brought a gun, Hilly. I'm so thankful, but what if you had shot someone? What if you had killed the man?"

Hilly with eyes wide, spoke in a shaky voice. "Oh, it's not loaded, baby. Lordy, I could never shoot anybody. I just threw the gun in my trunk last minute. After all, we's goin' west! But I didn't bring no bullets."

The two women broke into gales of laughter, the tension of the last hour finally dissipating. Britta pulled her lifelong friend into a hug. "What would I ever do without you, Hilly Durant?"

# Chapter 18

Back in Thatcher Springs, plans were coming together wonderfully for the family reunion! The women got together on a regular basis now, to discuss ideas, menus, activities, and the like. It was Millie, however, that stayed on top of the correspondence. She had written Cody and Lila of course, and Lila's folks, the Penroses, Ada and Will, Liz and Freddie, as well as Pearl and Gus—clear across the world in China. Although it was a long-shot that everyone could come, Millie prayed over each family, that all would make it. Of course, Josh and Joey would be there, she was sure. After all, they already lived in Oregon. Her twinners, she knew, wouldn't miss it for the world, wherever they had to come from.

With combined efforts, the women came up with a guest list—over thirty of the *immediate family*. "We will plan for at least a dozen extras, make sure there's plenty of food. It wouldn't surprise me a bit if Josh and Joe brought along lady friends." She chuckled at the thought of it.

Kate laughed out loud. Every time she thought of Josh and Joey, which was most the time, she pictured them still nine years old, their age when she first "found" them.

Millie had practically become pen pals with the interior decorator in Portland, who was thrilled with the plans for refurbishing the Inn at Seaside and helpful in other ways. The woman had arranged for a well-known photographer and offered to carry out errands, above and beyond the decorating contract. She had sent samples and diagrams, assuring, "The sky is the limit!" Millie had sent a sizeable down payment, assuring the sky was the limit from her end too, praise be to God.

The back door into the kitchen area creaked open. It was Silas with two-year-old Henry, Sam and Grace's youngest. His little voice shouted out the usual, "Gwamma Dahlin'?" Silas looked after him each morning while Grace taught school. Henry mimicked his grandpa's every word. "Me and Gwampa want coffee!" Millie jumped from where the ladies had been meeting. "I guess this meetin' is adjourned, for now anyway. I have a couple handsome men needin' me out in the kitchen!"

About the same time, Max came through the front door with little Max on his shoulders. "Speakin' of handsome men!" Kate exclaimed as she smiled up at her two Maxes. It didn't take her long to realize something was wrong. "What is it, Max?"

He pulled a letter out of his back pocket. "Pony Express tossed this off a bit ago, a letter from the boys." Kate jumped up from her chair. "Everything's all right, honey. Josh will be fine."

"What happened?" She was a breath away from a feeling of panic. "What's wrong with Josh?"

Millie and Silas, still holding little Henry, walked in from the kitchen with a fresh pot of coffee. Immediately Millie sensed something amiss. "What is it, Max?" She set the pot down.

"It's Josh. He got hurt, but he's gonna be all right. I'll just read the letter." He handed off the baby to Kate and suggested they all sit down. Everyone complied, but mostly on the edge of their chairs.

*January 2, 1877*

*Dear Max, Kate, Millie, Silas, Sam and Grace, Pierre, Simone, and all of you young'ins,*

*Happy New Year to our Thatcher Springs family! We miss y'all so much. We talk every day about the good times, the good food, and mostly the good people back home. We got Millie's letter about the family reunion. If anyone can make it happen, it's Miss Millie! We are doing fine, still working at McLemore Ranch and going to Baker Baptist. We've met some fine folks here. You'll probably find it out, so might as well tell ya I got me a girl (this is Joe talkin') and she's a keeper! Guess you'll meet her—Betsy—next July. Josh is writing the next part.*

*Hello, everyone. I don't exactly have me a girl like Joe but got a great little buddy, Jack Witherspoon. I'd like him to come to our reunion if y'all agree. His grandmother'll probably come too. Eula Mae. She's quite a lady herself. I had a little mishap, soon after we got to Baker, back in September. There was a bank holdup and wouldn't ya know I was in the bank? Got caught in the crossfire but my bullet wound is all healed up just fine. Guess the Lord planned it that way, so Joe and Betsy could get to know each other. The only thing, as old Henry would say, "I've got a hitch in my get-along." Ha ha.*

*Hope everyone there is doing good. We pray for y'all and know you are praying for us too.*

*We love you folks and miss you very much.*

*Josh and Joe*

———

Later that evening when the children were in bed, Kate and Max sat in front of the fire sipping coffee. "You're worried about Josh." It was a statement, not a question. Kate knew her husband well.

"It seems strange that we're just now hearin' about it. Josh got shot four months ago and nobody told us? And the thing about hitch in his get-along? What's that s'posed ta mean?"

"He probably didn't want us worryin'."

"I think it's worse than he let on. Maybe didn't plan on tellin' it at all, until they got Millie's letter about the reunion. Might be he's got a big scar or a limp. Somethin' like that."

"I pray for Josh and Joe every day, Max. Every day. When they took off on their own, I had to let them go, trust God. They're not boys anymore. They're learnin' to be men." There was a long pause. For all of Kate's wisdom, she burst into tears. "My poor little Josh. I can't believe he got shot!"

"He'll be fine, darlin'! One thing about our boys, they're made of tough stuff."

———

Britta was beginning to doubt her decision to go west. Her head hurt. The short-line train to eastern Oregon was terribly uncomfortable and dusty, their fancy Pullman car a thing of the past. She tried to get comfortable on the hard bench and go to sleep, but it was so cold. Hilly had pulled extra coats out of their trunks before they boarded; otherwise, they would be freezing.

The noise on their car was endless. Mothers were scolding rambunctious children; a baby wailed a few rows behind her. "You gonna be all right, Britta girl?" Hilly would do anything for Britta, but there was no denying she was spoiled. The child couldn't help it. Far as everyone knew, she was born into wealth. Hilly feared that Britta meeting her birth mother and twin sister would be difficult for her. Baker City was a long way from New York, in more ways than one.

"I should have listened to Mother." She started to cry. "I just wanta go home!"

Detective Crane had changed trains along with them and was seated in the back of their car. He walked past on several occasions, and when he noticed Britta in dire straits, he offered her a candy bar. Oddly it cheered her up a little. She hadn't realized she was hungry, the last stop offering a pathetic menu she declined to eat.

A few hours before their destination, Britta, with Hilly's help, redid her hair and tried to brush the dust from her traveling suit. She washed her face. By the time Hilly adjusted her "New York style" hat back on her head, tilted just so, she was feeling a bit better. *But Lord, I'm scared. Please be with me when I meet her. My sister.*

# Chapter 19

Betsy was nervous. Excited, but nervous. She wore her new blue dress and Eula Mae's cape. She had to pinch herself a few times. They were on their way to the train stop. Today, at last, she would meet her twin sister, Britta. *I'm scared Lord, please be with me when I meet her.*

Sloan and Betsy drove the buggy that would carry their guests, and Joe drove the wagon to haul their luggage. They had all pitched in preparing the best room for Britta and Hilda, that the boardinghouse had to offer. Sloan had made new curtains and purchased soft blue bed covers. She had prepared a big pot of soup early that simmered on the back of the stove and of course baked fresh bread and two pies, one huckleberry and one apple. Josh and Jack, along with Uncle Charlie and Eula Mae would set things up for supper in the kitchen with their guests.

"Oh my. Isn't this a wonderful day!" Eula Mae exclaimed. She had decided on the deep purple velvet with cream lace. "Charles, would you and Jackson bring in extra chairs please?" She spread a linen cloth on the table and began setting it with her own best china and silver that Jack had fetched from home. He had also brought a silver candelabra and candles which would serve as centerpiece. The lovely table, mismatched chairs and all, was in sharp contrast to the utilitarian kitchen, Sloan's workshop. Everyone wanted the best for Britta Lundgren.

———

The train was an hour late, but no one was surprised by it. Jangled nerves became even more jangled for the waiting. Betsy and Sloan paced the empty platform where passengers would disembark. Joe tended the horses and tried to calm the women. Betsy stopped suddenly. "Listen!" She put a hand to her ear. "It's coming."

The train finally approached, slowing, screeching to a halt in a hissing cloud of steam. Porters swung out from two doors, even before the train fully stopped, setting out stepstools to assist departing passengers. Trunks were unloaded and stacked on the platform. Several weary travelers stepped down; a mother with three children greeted their papa happily. Two rough-looking individuals, probably miners, appeared, lighting a smoke. Next came a dapper gentleman who looked a bit out of place. He did a double take of Betsy, tipped his hat, and continued walking by. That seemed to be the last of the passengers. Sloan grabbed Betsy's hand; Joe was already holding the other one. All three were thinking the same thing: *Britta is not on the train.* Betsy's heart was about to sink when all at once, she appeared, Britta, standing in the doorway as if she couldn't take another step. She wore a deep blue traveling suit trimmed in black, a fancy black hat, and kid gloves. A strong voice from behind her encouraged, "Go on now, baby."

Betsy left the security of her mother and Joe, walking slowly toward her sister. She was suddenly aware of her plainness compared to Britta. At the same time, she was awestruck. *She looks just like me!*

Britta must have been thinking the same thing because the look on her face was that of astonishment. They just stood there looking at each other until Hilly broke the tense moment. "Well, glory be! You gotta be Miss Betsy McLemore!" She wrapped Betsy in a big hug, laughing heartily.

Sloan stepped forward embracing Hilda Durant, the woman who had delivered her babies, so long ago. Then she turned toward Britta, reaching for her hand. She couldn't hold back happy tears. "You are beautiful Britta, simply beautiful!" She sniffed, trying to collect her emotions. Failing to do so, she pulled Britta into a warm hug. "Thank you so very much for coming. It will get easier, honey," Sloan promised.

Joe and the local stationmaster hauled the ladies' trunks to the wagon. The three large ones were tagged "Miss Lundgren," and one smaller trunk was for "Hilda Durant." Joe strode over to the four women. He looked at Britta and then at Betsy, then back again at Britta. "Well, I'll be jiggered. Twins! I've never in all my life seen identical twins!" He shook his head in fake bewilderment as Betsy whacked him on the arm. They looked at each other knowingly and broke out laughing.

Britta had no idea of course that Joe was a twin himself. She wasn't in on the obviously private joke. "Do you think we could go ahead to our quarters? I'm looking forward to a nap and a hot bath before dinner is served." Everyone turned toward her, a look of reservation on their faces. *She's a snooty little thing*, Joe thought.

---

As they gathered in the kitchen for supper, Sloan introduced Britta and Hilly to Uncle Charlie, Eula Mae, Jackson, and Josh, who had pulled up to the table in his wheelchair. Hilly laughed and said, "Don't tell me! Another set of twins? There some kinda twin convention in this town?" Everyone laughed. Britta smiled, acting nonchalant about the whole thing.

Despite Betsy and Britta not yet warming up to one another as Sloan had hoped and prayed, the mood was comfortable, Hilly joking with Jack, pointing out his good manners. Of course, everyone commented on the delicious meal, thanking Sloan.

Having Uncle Charlie and Eula Mae at the table was a godsend. Not only did they temper the atmosphere with their light-hearted conversation, Josh observed a spark between the two. He was smiling to himself about the wonder of it, when he glanced up to see Britta looking right at him. She quickly looked down at her soup.

When they all sat back, satisfied with Sloan's hearty meal, Betsy jumped up and said, "Just relax everyone. I'll serve the pie." It was unanimous; they all wanted a little slice of each. Hilly offered to help, but Betsy wouldn't have it. "You're our guest, Miss Durant! I want to serve you."

Britta was taken back in a way. It had never occurred to her to serve Hilly. Even so, she was beginning to relax a bit, feeling better after the meal. Britta drew comfort from being at the kitchen table, bringing thoughts of her grandmother. Except for Eula Mae, who seemed more dignified, the "family" appeared to be of lower-class workers. Though she kept quiet about it, she was not only staggered that she was sitting there with her identical twin sister, but that Josh and Joe were twins too. Why one was wheelchair bound piqued her curiosity. *I wonder what happed to him.* Britta was determined to find out.

# Chapter 20

About the time of the split-pea soup fire in Witherspoon's kitchen, Miss Brown, the Baker City schoolteacher, resigned from her position due to chronic headaches. At least that's what she claimed. Everybody knew it was the Riley boys. Eula Mae had decided she would tutor Jackson herself, once they were settled in the boardinghouse.

After Christmas holidays, school reopened—subject to weather—with a new headmaster, Mr. Fitzsimmons. Jack began the trek back to school. He recognized right off that the new teacher was stricter than Miss Brown had been. Jack was a good student, respectful, and got along well with everyone. Frank and Chester Riley didn't get along with anybody. They were notorious bullies.

Jack came home early one day with a note from the teacher, for his "parents." He walked into Josh's room and was just about to share the trouble, when Britta knocked on the open door. "May I come in?"

"Sure," Josh said. "Us men are just shootin' the bull."

She looked a bit put off, but ignored the comment. "It's pretty quiet around her today," she mused. "Most everyone went to Eula Mae's house I guess, to clean up after the carpenters."

Josh chuckled. "Well, ya see, it was the split-pea soup that started it all." He looked at Jack and winked. "The wood handle on Eula Mae's spoon caught fire—that happened just after we got here."

"Grandmother forgot about it," Jack explained, "the soup. The smoke nearly choked us to death, made our eyes water and smelled terrible." He wrinkled up his nose, making a frightful face.

Britta smiled and nodded. Out of the blue, she turned toward Josh. She was standing near the foot of the bed. "What happened to you?"

He shot a look at Jack. "Just a little mishap. Took a bullet last September. It's pretty much healed up." Josh tried to sound unconcerned.

Jack interjected, "He stepped in front of Mrs. Smith and her baby in a bank robbery! Saved their lives. He won't tell ya himself, but he's a hero in Baker City."

Josh glared at Jack. "What about that note y'all brung home, Jackson?"

"Oh nothin really. Mr. Fitsimmons the new teacher, just wants to meet my parents. Today."

Britta continued her meddling. "Are you paralyzed because of it? Is that the reason you're in a wheelchair? Lying in bed?"

Josh gave her a look that conveyed it wasn't any of her business. He ignored her questions. "So Jack, did ya get in trouble at school?" He couldn't imagine it possible.

Jack was about to excuse himself so he wouldn't have to answer in front of Miss Lundgren, when the others returned. They burst through the back door, rubbing their hands together, everyone headed for the stove. It had begun to snow.

———

Mr. Fitzsimmons cleared his throat, and looked very serious as he addressed Jackson Witherspoon's guardians, Mrs. Witherspoon and Mr. Reed. "A new student joined us recently. His name is Jose Gomez. Well, he goes by 'Lefty.' Poor chap lost his right arm." He went on describing how the Riley boys had harassed Lefty, since the day he arrived.

Eula Mae looked concerned. "Why those naughty boys!" she exclaimed. "But what has this got to do with Jackson?"

"Today the boys went outdoors during dinner hour to play in the snow. Frank and Chet—the Rileys—I understand, were bullying Lefty, who is only nine, calling him names, slamming snowballs at close range. When I walked out to call them back to class, everyone but the Riley boys returned." Mr. Fitzsimmons paused, looking directly at Jack, his mouth twitching as if holding back a smile. "I heard some commotion behind the building and discovered Frank and Chet, roped and tied back to back, cursing at the snow piled on their heads."

Josh was beginning to get the picture. He turned to Jack. "You roped 'em?" He broke into a wide grin. "That's impressive! Er, I mean—shame on you, Jackson Witherspoon." Even trying to sound stern, Josh couldn't get the smile off his face.

Eula Mae clasped her hands together. "Oh my!"

Mr. Fitzsimmons went on, speaking to Jack. "Perhaps you should leave your rope at home, son. But I must commend you for defending young Lefty Gomez, especially against two bigger and older boys. You have courage and compassion." He looked at Eula Mae. "You are doing a fine job raising your grandson, Mrs. Witherspoon." He turned to face Josh. "And how are *you* involved with Jackson, Mr. Reed?"

"Well," Josh began, but Jack interrupted.

"He's my good buddy, sir. It was Josh that taught me how to rope!"

---

Betsy slipped down to the kitchen to make a cup of cocoa. Everyone had gone to bed, but she was restless. To her surprise, Britta was there looking through the cupboards. They startled each other. "Oh!" Britta exclaimed. "I was wanting to make some cocoa."

"Me too," said Betsy. "Here. It's over here." Betsy stirred up the fire and added a few pieces of kindling. She quickly got a small pan of milk on to heat.

"Thank you. Hilly usually brings it to me." Britta laughed, embarrassed. "I don't actually know how to make it."

"It's okay. I come down to the kitchen often at night. Ya know, when I can't sleep."

"I can't sleep either." She laughed nervously. "Hilly snores."

The two pulled chairs close to the fire, sipping on their cocoa, the place quiet as a tomb.

Britta broke the silence. "What happened to him? Joshua."

For the next hour Betsy shared everything, from the day Josh and Joe Reed came into the café where she worked. She told her about that September morning when Josh offered to go to the bank, so Joe could spend extra time with her. How Josh was shot in the back during a robbery. She tried to explain how being around them, observing their love for each other, had nearly broken Sloan's heart. "It must've been so hard on her, the secret she carried for seventeen years. That's why I wrote ya, Britta. I know it's turned your world upside down. Mine too."

"And Joe?" Britta asked. "He's courting you?"

Betsy smiled brightly, her cheeks flushed. "Can ya keep a secret? Nobody knows, but me and Joe are gettin' hitched in June. He's gonna build us a cabin—out at the ranch. Don't tell, okay?"

———

The shared secret put a chink in Britta's armor. Later that week, the sisters ended up in the kitchen again, after everyone had turned in. This time Betsy showed Britta how to make cocoa. Britta got the fire crackling—all by herself. They sat comfortably, talking, but still with a trace of reservation. Betsy asked about New York, what all Britta did there.

"Well, my father is a doctor, and Mother—I guess, you would call a party giver! She's very into the social life." Britta smiled thinking about the difference between Alecia and Sloan. "I've assisted Father since I was twelve or even younger, at his clinic and now at the new hospital." She went on sharing some of her experience. "In those early years, Father treated victims from the war. Men who had lost limbs, some paralyzed." She thought of Josh but didn't say anything. "I plan to be a doctor myself one day. In fact, I've been accepted to medical school." She tried not to sound like she was boasting. "It starts in September."

Betsy's eyes were huge as she stared at her sister. "You must be very smart," she said with admiration. "And courageous," she added.

Britta nodded her thanks. Thoughts of little Liu filled her mind, and for a moment, she considered telling Betsy about the whole thing. "Well, I'm not always very courageous. Sometimes it's hard."

# Chapter 21

Eula Mae, Sloan, Josh, and Jack had just said their last amen after sunrise service one morning, when Britta appeared at the doorway. The sun rose later and later as the winter weeks went by, and some mornings clouds prevailed. But this day had blessed them with an extraordinary sunrise. "Oh my!" exclaimed Eula Mae as always. Then she noticed Britta. "Do come in, darling! The Lord just greeted us with a lovely sunrise."

Britta thought she might have been the first one up, but here they all were fully dressed for the day, Eula Mae in a fetching rust colored ensemble. Sloan was in her housedress and apron, wonderful smells already coming from the oven and Jack with his hair slicked back, was ready for school. Only Josh was in his pajamas, in bed, in need of a shave.

One by one they departed, back to their day, leaving Britta standing there a distance from Josh's bedside. He motioned to the rocker. "Have a seat," he offered, but not with much enthusiasm. He was curious though what "Miss Bratty" was doing there. That's what he and Jack secretly called the snooty little thing.

She cleared her throat. "Betsy told me about what happened. About the bank holdup and all."

He nodded and quipped, "Well, it *was* a bit of a distraction that day. Plumb forgot what I went to the bank for." He chuckled. He could tell she didn't think it was funny. She had something on her mind.

"Mr. Reed," she began, "I think I might be able to help you."

He laughed. "Doc Cartwright has done everything possible. This kind of thing just takes time. And by the way—call me Josh." He was becoming a bit irritated.

"I've had experience with paralysis, and sometimes positive results, using physical therapy."

"So, you think you're a doctor?" he asked with a bit of sarcasm.

"Well, I've worked alongside my father over the past five years," she said defensively. "He has many success stories, mostly victims of the war. Some that were never expected to walk again because of their injuries." Her voice had grown stronger, driving home her point. "I've also worked in the rehabilitation part of Providence Hospital. And—I've been accepted to medical school."

"Look, Miss Lundgren," his jaw tightened, "I've made peace with my fate. You need ta get on with your doctorin' somewhere else!"

She stood, color creeping up her neck. "I only want to help, Mr. Reed. You can lay in bed the rest of your life if you choose. It's no matter to me!"

Josh was downright mad by now. "Oh. So you want me to jump up and dance a jig?" he asked with jaws clenched.

Britta turned on her heal and stormed from the room, slamming the door behind her.

Josh stared at the closed door, seething. His empty coffee cup was still in his hand from a happier time this morning. He threw it with all his strength, shattering it against the closed door.

———

Later that night, "What's goin' on down here?" Sloan was surprised to see Betsy and Britta in the kitchen late one night, enjoying big mugs of cocoa. "You girls have trouble sleepin'?"

They looked at each other and laughed. "Wanta join us, Mama? Here. Sit here." Betsy jumped up. "I'll get another chair."

Sloan had heard Betsy slip downstairs and decided to join her. A winter storm was slamming sleet against the windows, howling winds, causing shutters to bang alongside the house. She wouldn't have been surprised to find others up and about because of it, yet she *was* surprised to see Britta sitting in the kitchen with Betsy.

Betsy poured cocoa for her mother, more for Britta and herself, and sat down.

Before she knew it, Sloan realized she was sitting between her two daughters, and much to her pleasure, the conversation seemed easy, comfortable. "Hope I didn't interrupt," she began.

"Maybe you can give some advice, Mama. Britta was just telling me about her grapple with Josh." Betsy looked at Britta reassuringly as if to say, "It's okay to speak your mind to Mama."

Britta began slowly. "I'm not a doctor. I know that. But there are some things … Maybe I can help him." The more she talked the more energized she became. "There are methods, physical therapy. If he wasn't so stubborn and obstinate, pig-headed!"

Sloan and Betsy both smothered their laughter that Britta was so riled up over Josh. "He's struggling," Sloan offered. "He's mastered that wheelchair, but it's as if he's given up. The Reed boys are strong in character; their faith runs deep. Josh puts on a brave front, but deep inside, he's hurting. Deep inside he's maybe even angry with God."

They talked for another hour, with Britta growing in her respect of Sloan. It was well after midnight when they said their goodnights. "I have an idea," Sloan said, "Why don't we see if Hilly is willing to make a trade? Let me be her roommate, and you girls share a room. That way, you can talk all night if you wish!"

Several days had passed, Britta avoiding contact of any kind with Josh. Even at dinner her attention was on Betsy or Jack or Uncle Charlie or Sloan's milk gravy, but never did she cast a glance at Josh.

Hilly could sense a change in Britta. She was growing comfortable with the family, even to the point of helping Betsy serve dessert after supper each night. She noticed Britta had softened her look too, especially since sharing a room with Betsy. Her hair was pinned up, but loosely, and she wore the simplest of dresses, although still a long shot from Betsy's calico.

That evening as Britta placed a slice of pie in front of Josh, he put a hand on her arm and looked up at her awkwardly. Their eyes held for a moment, then Britta moved quickly away as if he had the plague.

Later that night, when the boardinghouse was quiet, the sisters, together, knocked on Josh's door. Britta had been convinced that she needed to apologize and asked Betsy to come with her. They had rehearsed what Britta would say. She was truly sorry she had upset him, but still convinced she could help, if he would give her the chance.

Josh was reading by the lamplight. "Well," he said, "how lucky can a guy get?" A hint of sarcasm laced his voice.

Britta forgot the words of apology she had rehearsed. "I just want to try, Josh. Give me a chance."

Betsy chimed in, "Just give her a chance. What have you got to lose?"

Britta pressed on. "If we can get the blood circulating, fire up some of those muscles, there might be a possibility—"

Josh cut her off. "Look, Miss Britta." *Why is she so irritating?* He went on, "I know you mean well, but—"

She cut him off. "Precisely."

Betsy broke in again. "Try it, Josh. Don't be so stubborn and pig-headed!"

Britta stared at Betsy, her blue eyes huge.

Just then, Sloan walked in. She folded her arms looking at Josh. "Betsy's right. Don't be so pig-headed."

Eula Mae appeared at the door. "Oh my! How lovely. A late night gathering of the saints!"

Betsy didn't skip a beat. "I'll get the cocoa."

# Chapter 22

Nearly a week passed by before Josh saw Britta again. He was beginning to think she had changed her mind about the physical therapy. On Saturday morning, however, Joe walked in hauling two long pieces of pipe, followed by Jack with an armload of two-by-fours. "We're just following instructions from Miss Br—" He almost said *Bratty*, but then Britta walked in, carrying leather straps. Hans, the carpenter, followed her, his arms loaded with supplies.

"What in the world?" Josh didn't like the looks of things.

Britta hardly acknowledged him in her exuberance, giving orders to the whole crew. "We'll need to shove the bed up tight to the window wall, and clear out space over here." She was in her glory, transforming Josh's room into the "rehabilitation unit" of Mrs. Bush's boardinghouse.

Jack was recruited as Britta's assistant and she showed him how to manipulate Josh's feet, bending, twisting, and holding in different positions. At the same time, Britta worked on Josh's back, pressing and pushing against one vertebra at a time. She applied extra pressure around the wound area, which made him flinch, but overall he decided this physical therapy business was quite nice. Even though Jack was putting all his strength into it, Josh felt nothing in his feet.

All the while, Joe and Hans were busy constructing the "walking bars" and frames that would be bolted to the floor, positioned over the bed. Betsy was sewing a padded cover to be secured on the horizontal board. Sloan's contribution was the new flannel pajamas she had sewn for Josh. He only wished the fabric didn't feature kittens.

"It will take time, Josh." Britta sounded optimistic at the end of the week. "Thank you for agreeing to this. I know it's hard and maybe discouraging. Sunday, we rest, then next week the hot water bottles should be here—I ordered from the mercantile." She plopped down in the rocking chair looking weary. "Mind if I have a sip?" She took a drink of water from his glass on the bed table.

Josh was watching her—quiet. After a while he said flatly, "You look like Betsy."

"We're *twins*," she said and rolled her eyes. Then explained, "I didn't bother with makeup today."

He kept looking at her. She had worked so hard at trying to help him. Did she care? Or was it her ego? Out of the blue he asked, "Why'd ya come out here? Ta Oregon?"

She looked at him, perplexed. "Isn't it obvious? I wanted to meet my family. Betsy wrote a letter. Invited me."

"But you didn't have to come. With your *profession* and all." There was a hint of sarcasm in his voice. "What made you decide?"

There was a long stretch of silence between them. They were there alone, just the two of them, as Jack had been excused to go out and practice roping. Britta seemed a mile away, lost in her thoughts. She didn't look at him. "There was a little girl. A tiny Chinese girl." Josh could barely hear her. "She was brought into the hospital with other children, gathered from the streets of Brooklyn." There was a long pause as she struggled with her emotions. Josh waited. "She had lived with her sister in the streets, in horrible conditions. A child should never have to live like that!" A single tear slipped down her cheek. "All she wanted was her sister. I couldn't tell her that her sister had died." More tears came. "The sister was eleven and little Liu only four." A sob escaped. "I said tomorrow morning I will come early with a present—just for you. I thought it would give her hope."

Britta was full out crying now, dabbing at her eyes with a hanky. "But when I got there, her bed was empty, made up for the next patient." She was shaking her head in disbelief all over again. She buried her face in her hands.

When finally, she looked up at Josh, his hand was extended, palm open. Slowly she reached out, placing her hand in his. "I'm so sorry, Britta," he said softly, holding her trembling hand with his strong one. "God knows."

---

Three weeks had passed since Britta and Hilly arrived in Baker City. Hilly brought the subject up at dinner one evening. "My goodness, how the days are flyin' by! I've been havin' such a wonderful time with all you folks." She looked around the table, smiling at each one. "Less than a week left!"

Britta shot a glance at Josh. She looked a bit pale. "A week, Hilly?" She hadn't realized it.

Betsy spoke up. "Well, couldn't ya stay a little longer? We haven't gone out to the ranch yet. And Doc Cartwright was wantin' ya ta be here for the hospital inauguration." Betsy looked down at her plate. "I really want ya ta stay, Britta."

"Me too." Sloan looked at her daughter lovingly.

"C'mon, Britta. Ya still got work ta do!" exclaimed Joe as he nodded toward Josh.

Uncle Charlie chimed in. "We all want ya ta stay. Right, everbody?"

"Oh my. It would be so lovely to have you here for—uh, a little longer, Britta dear."

Jack said, "Me and Josh need ya, Miss Britta. For physical therapy."

Britta glanced across the table at Josh in his wheelchair. He didn't say anything, just looked at her, his brown eyes imploring, *Please stay.*

---

Work at the ranch had come to a halt after a huge snowfall, giving Joe more time in town. More time with Josh, even to the point of following Britta's therapy instruction. Josh, with the strength of his upper body and the wood supports bolted to the floor, was now able to get from his bed to the wheelchair on his own. He still had no feeling in his legs, but knew more independence in that one accomplishment.

After school one day, Jack knocked on Josh's open door. Usually he just walked in, but today he had brought a friend home with him. Lefty Gomez. Josh automatically reached out with his right hand and Lefty didn't hesitate to shake with his left. "What you fellas up to?"

"Well, since it's a pretty good day for it, Lefty wants to learn to rope." Jack spoke with confidence, as if he didn't notice that Lefty only had one arm.

Josh shot a glance at Joe. "I see," he said. "How 'bout you boys find Miss Sloan? Maybe she can rustle up some milk and cookies, and I'll meet ya out back in twenty minutes."

Lefty Gomez was the youngest of seven boys, a total surprise to his parents, Pedro and Juanita. His father was foreman of one of the biggest outfits in the area, and four of his brothers worked there as hands. The other two worked for a logging company. Because of his handicap, Juanita worried that Jose wouldn't be able to work like his brothers. She and Pedro decided that Jose should be in school. In September, she and her son moved into a tiny apartment above the Home Cookin" Café. Juanita had been happy to learn at the time that the waitress job had just been vacated. By now, mid-February, she understood why. She would put up with the cantankerous cook, only until school was out.

Josh was amazed at the young man's dexterity and how he made the best of his handicap. His right arm had been amputated just above the elbow when he was three. "My padre say, 'No, no! Don't reach in there!' But I was after a rabbit." He chuckled. "Instead, I caught a snake."

It didn't take him long, not as long as it had taken Jack, to rope the dummy steer. His left arm was strong and accurate; what remained of his right easily held the rope.

Hilly was grinning from ear to ear as she watched from the porch, bundled in Eula Mae's fur coat. *What a sight, Lord. You sure have a way of bringin' folks together.* She shook her head at the scene: Josh in a wheelchair, Jose Gomez, a happy one-armed Mexican boy, and Jack Witherspoon, taking care of everybody.

After that, Lefty was a regular. He came home with Jack every afternoon. When his mama had to work late, he was invited to stay for supper. One evening as the family gathered together, Sloan brought up the ranch. She hoped to spend more time out there, somehow work only part-time at the boardinghouse. "Uncle Charlie and Joe here have gotten the place in such good shape. I spoke with Mr. Abernathy at the bank, and he agreed to a loan, so I can buy a small herd of cows. I just need to find a cook to replace me here—at the boardinghouse."

Joe and Betsy lit up at the idea, looking at each other. They hadn't shared their secret yet.

Uncle Charlie and Eula Mae seemed all for it too, smiling at each other.

Little Lefty spoke up. "My madre is very good cook! She makes the best tamales." It was the first they had heard that his mother was working at Home Cookin'.

"Your mama works *there*?" Betsy asked, a look of distress on her face.

"Si. But she don't like the cook."

# Chapter 23

Alecia had to lie down when she received word that Britta wished to stay another month. Nothing would console her. "I was afraid this would happen!" She cried as if Britta was never coming home.

"She's making progress with a patient, sweetheart. Surely you can understand," Edward explained. "She'll be home before Easter."

"Well, I could certainly use Hilly!" She sobbed. Alecia could be overdramatic.

"Hilly needs to stay with her, dear." Edward had not disclosed Detective Crane's report about the train robbery, Britta's brief captivity. "Perhaps you would consider traveling to Oregon?"

She looked at her husband, stunned. "That's not remotely possible, Edward. There's Winter Tea and then the Valentine's Ball. And what of recital? Impossible. Britta must come home."

———

Dr. Cartwright was quite intrigued with Britta's methods of rehabilitation. He kept tabs on the progress. Though slow, there seemed to be some improvement in Josh's mobility. He could get from his bed into the wheelchair and wheel himself to the walking bars. In the beginning, it took Britta, Joe, and Jack to assist him from wheelchair to standing, but in less than two weeks, Josh could manage the whole procedure on his own, bed to wheelchair to bars to standing. He would carry out the routine several times a day, even after everyone had gone to bed. The standing part was by the strength of his arms—at first. Slowly but surely, even though he still had no feeling in his legs, he would let his hands relax until he was standing on his own, barely holding the bars.

Britta's first goal was to get the blood circulating through Josh's body, blood to his idle muscles. The trouble was, ever since that night when she had told him about the little Chinese girl, things felt different between them. The way he had held her hand. His brown eyes, sympathetic. Now, when she was working on his spine, instead of concentrating on each vertebra, she noticed how broad his shoulders were. At times, when she was adjusting the padded boards that would keep his legs positioned a certain way, she would look up to see him gazing at her. She also realized he no longer seemed to be angry over the whole thing, no longer spoke with sarcasm.

———

Joe and Uncle Charlie had the buckboard sleigh ready, the horses hitched-up and hay bales positioned for everyone's comfort. They had all looked forward to this Sunday, a day at the ranch. Joe and Betsy rode ahead, horseback, to build a fire, get the house warmed up. Uncle Charlie drove the team and Eula Mae rode shotgun. She had chosen the brown tweed traveling suit to complement her beaver coat and matching hat. It was not lost on Jack that Uncle Charlie and Eula Mae were quite snuggled, wrapped in a plaid wool blanket. He nudged Josh, nodding in their direction. Both stifled a snicker. Lefty sat between them, happy as a clam, smiling his infectious smile. Across from them, Sloan, Britta, and Hilly huddled together, in a pile of quilts, laughing as they glided along on packed snow. Sloan started singing a folk tune, and before long, everyone else joined in. Britta was having a wonderful time; she was happy. Whenever she glanced up, Josh was looking at her. For a minute, she imagined sitting by him, nestled together in warm blankets.

———

Sloan put a pot of stew on the stove, while Hilly and Eula Mae formed rolls from the chilled yeast dough she had prepared earlier. Charlie was holding a "workshop" on saddle making for Josh and the boys, while Joe suggested he and Betsy give Britta a tour of the ranch. "That would be great!" exclaimed Britta. I haven't ridden for months." Now that they were at the ranch, she was very glad she hadn't worn the English riding gear packed in her trunk. Thanks to Betsy, the girls were both dressed in britches, shirts, wool sweaters, neckerchiefs, and boots, all on top of warm, somewhat itchy, long-johns.

As the sisters pulled on jackets and deer-hide gloves, Sloan came out of the back room with a well-worn cowboy hat and popped it on Britta's head. Betsy had her own hat. Hilly was busting up laughing. "If Miss Alecia could only see ya now, baby. Oh lands! She be havin' a fit."

The sun had broken through snow clouds, turning the whole ranch into an enchanted place. Icicles three feet long hung from the roof and acres of sparkling white in every direction caused their eyes to squint. Joe had the three horses saddled: his, Betsy's, and Uncle Charlie's. Betsy offered Patches' reins to Britta. "Here Britta, take my horse, Patches. He's a sweetheart."

Britta looked doubtful as she examined him front to back. "Does he jump?"

Betsy and Joe looked at each other. "Only when necessary," said Betsy in a serious tone, then she and Joe burst out laughing. "Or when he's scared!" Joe exclaimed, and they erupted in another round of laughter. Betsy and Joe played off each other like that. Betsy slapped her leg. "That was a good one." Britta shot a look of aversion at them, rolling her eyes.

Later, when the sisters burst through the door, their cheeks red as apples, they were laughing like best friends. "That was amazing!" Britta exclaimed. She peeled off her coat, tossed her hat on a peg, and walked right over to Josh. Placing a hand on his shoulder, her blue eyes sparkling she announced, "Before long, you'll be going with us, Josh." He looked up at her from where he was seated in the rocking chair. There seemed a silent message between them. Hope rekindled. The family looked their way, each one somber for a fleeting moment, then back to their busyness.

After dinner and before pie, Eula Mae stood and cleared her throat. "I would like to make an announcement," she began, to everyone's surprise. Her cheeks turned pink. From across the table, Jack's eyes grew big. He and Josh looked at each other. The chatter and laughter stopped, the room quiet except for wood crackling in the stove. Eula Mae cleared her throat again. "Your presence is requested next Sunday, at four o'clock, at Baker Baptist Church." She looked lovingly at Uncle Charlie. "Charles and I," she cleared her throat and began again, "Charles Alexander and I are getting hitched!"

Just like they were kids again, Josh and Joe looked at each other. "Will wonders never cease!" they said in unison. Then everyone erupted with their congratulations, happy laughter filling the house.

Jack whispered to Josh, "Mark my words: she's gonna break out the pink chiffon."

---

After their day at the ranch, Betsy and Britta were much more easy-going around each other. Britta, suddenly was fun to be with. They were caught whispering and laughing, often finishing the other's sentences. The two were acting more like twins every day.

They were getting ready for bed one evening, Britta brushing her hair and Betsy jumping on the bed, tossing a pillow in the air. Britta wanted to have a chat about Josh, but Betsy was just being

Betsy. "Sometimes you act so immature! Can't we just sit down like big girls and have a conversation?" To Britta's disbelief, a pillow came out of nowhere and hit her on the head! "What in the world?"

Betsy jumped down from the bed, grabbed the pillow, and hit her again. "Ya never had a pillow fight?"

Britta quickly got the idea and grabbed her own pillow, swinging it wildly at Betsy. Before long the two girls were causing a ruckus, smacking each other with fat downy pillows, squealing with laughter. Just before Sloan opened the door to see what the commotion was, one of the pillows split open, filling the room with downy white feathers. Betsy twirled around as if she was in magic land, while Britta frantically jumped up and down, spitting feathers.

Sloan couldn't help herself. She started laughing. When they saw her, the girls started laughing too, until all three could barely stand up. They tried catching feathers with their hands and scooping them into the pillowcase. Sloan attempted gathering them in her apron. Feathers were stuck on their faces and in their hair. Every move they made caused a whirlwind of feathers. They couldn't quit laughing. Trying to be quiet for the sake of sleeping boarders only made matters worse.

A distant shout grabbed their attention. "Did you hear that?" Sloan asked in a whisper.

From somewhere below, it came again. "Britta! Britta!" It was Josh. All three women tore down the stairs, a flurry of feathers going with them as they rushed into Josh's room.

"What is it, Josh? What's wrong?" Britta had stopped abruptly at the foot of his bed, Betsy and Sloan colliding behind her.

Josh was smiling with tears streaking his face. "I thought there was somethin in my bed," he explained. "A varmint or somethin'." He laughed, shaking his head. "It was my foot, Britta. I can feel my foot!"

Britta rushed into Josh's arms crying her thanks to the Lord. They embraced with silent understanding and then remembering Sloan and Betsy in the room, Britta stood trying to recover her emotions. In a shaky voice, she said, "I am so proud of you, Josh. You've been working so hard."

Everyone came for sunrise service the next morning. Josh looked around the room at these dear folks who had faithfully prayed for him, had waited on him hand and foot. Eula Mae and Uncle Charlie, Hilly, his buddy Jack, Miss Sloan, a godsend, sweet Betsy, and most of all his brother Joe. They had given so much for him.

And then there was Britta. The snooty little thing from New York City, the least expected, turned out to have the most determination and faith in him. "I love you all," he said, and meant it with his whole heart.

## Chapter 24

It took the women all day Saturday (keeping Eula Mae out of the kitchen) to prepare for the wedding feast. Cake would be served at the church and afterward, a big family dinner in the boardinghouse kitchen. Turned out Hilly was an accomplished cake maker and spent hours on details of the three-tiered creation. Britta had no clue on food preparation, but Sloan set her to kneading dough for dinner rolls. "Just pretend it's Josh's back," Betsy whispered in her ear. A flour fight nearly ensued, but Sloan wisely called Betsy to another task.

Eula Mae looked regal in her pink chiffon gown, off the shoulders no less, the skirt billowing. For seventy something (no one knew for sure) her posture was perfect and her silver hair pulled back in a fancy twist complemented her soft skin and rosy cheeks. Her eyes danced as she took Charlie's hand. He had fashioned a new leather vest for the occasion, but otherwise was dressed in classic "Uncle Charlie."

Josh in his wheelchair, alongside Joe and Jack, "stood" by Charlie, and Sloan, Betsy, and Britta by Eula Mae. Happy tears were shed for the newlyweds. Even Britta's cheeks were streaked with moisture. When at last, the preacher pronounced them husband and wife, Jack spoke up offering a hand to the groom. "Well then,

Uncle Charlie, guess this means you're my grandpa now!" Everyone laughed as Charlie hugged the boy, chuckling happiness.

There hadn't been a wedding at Baker Baptist for ages and the congregation did not want the party to end. Sloan said something to the girls and then Joe and the four discreetly slipped out. "We've gotta get back to the kitchen, Joe. Could ya drive us home?" She was nervous about the elk roast in the oven and had to get the pot of peeled potatoes on the stove, set the table, take out the roast if it was done, make the gravy, and put in the rolls. They had left in a hurry, leaving pots and pans piled in the sink.

Before they opened the back door, wonderful aromas filled the air, something Sloan didn't quite recognize. To their amazement, the kitchen was spotless! The table was beautifully set, the roast, covered with a linen, sat on the warming shelf, and the potatoes bubbled away on the back of the stove. They could smell the rolls baking in the oven. "They're here, Madre," Lefty Gomez announced.

As the three walked in, a plump Mexican woman turned from her mission at the stove, laughing robustly. She had a beautiful face with wide brown eyes. Her black hair was pulled into a neat bun and her big smile revealed a silver tooth. She opened her arms toward them. "My name ees Juanita. Jose here, he tell me you folks need cook? I cook for you. Everything ees ready! Tonight we have tamales!"

———

Back at Thatcher Springs, Millie had received word from everyone, except Gus and Pearl. "It's not likely they'll come," she said to Silas with a tone of sadness in her voice.

"Well, there's a big ocean between Chiner and Oregon, honey. It's just amazin' everbody else is comin'." He wrapped his arms around her waist as she washed their breakfast dishes. "Yer purty amazin' yerself, Millie darlin'. I'm so proud of you for puttin' the whole shebang together!"

"I hope so. That it comes together. There's a million details ta this thing." Millie sounded weary.

Just then, Kate popped through the back door. "Millie! It's a letter from Pearl!"

"Well, bless Pat! We were just talkin' about them." The three scrambled to sit at the table, while Kate read the letter.

*March 2, 18 77*

*Our dear Thatcher Springs family,*

*We are coming! Gus just found out we've been given a furlough from mid-May until the end of September. We are excited to see you all and have so much to share from our home in China. God is moving in powerful ways. Gus and I love our work here.*

*Millie, we are bringing you a beautiful present from China!*

*Can't wait to see you all!*

*With love,*
*Pearl*

Millie couldn't help shed a happy tear. "That means *everyone* is comin! Oh, thank you, Lord."

"What d'ya suppose the present is?" Silas noticed Millie was back to her old self.

"Maybe some a that Cloisonné they make over there." She smiled. "But the real present is they're comin!"

The manager at Seaside Inn had assured Millie her grocery list would be ordered and stored in the cooler, ready for their arrival. The interior designer in Portland was happy to have her assistant purchase and wrap gifts for all the children. Millie, with help from Grace and Kate, looked through catalogues to figure it all out. There would be kites for the older ones, beach balls and little tin buckets with shovels for the young ones. None of them had ever seen a sandy beach, let alone the ocean!

The refurbishing of Seaside Inn would be complete by June 1. The train tickets had been purchased for everyone. Rooms at the Grand Hotel in San Francisco had been reserved for their layover where Ike and Esther Penrose would join them for the last leg of their journey. Millie felt quite sure nothing could go wrong.

---

It had been nothing short of a miracle, that the feeling had returned to Josh's feet. Britta was so energized, ready to try advanced therapy. She sent a second wire to New York City, to let her parents know it would be another two weeks—at least.

With one foot at a time, she instructed him to push against the padded plank as she and Jack put all their strength in pushing back, giving resistance. It was difficult and painful. "C'mon, buddy," Jack encouraged.

Sweat beaded his forehead. "Push!" Britta didn't let up. "C'mon, Josh. Once more."

The next phase took place at the bars. Josh easily went from his bed to the wheelchair, over to the bars, and lifted himself to standing, holding to the bars. "Just stand there for a few minutes, then we're going to try something new." Britta was all business until she caught his eyes, his deep brown eyes looking directly into hers. She swallowed, unable to look away.

"Thank you, Britta," he said softly. "I know you were s'posed ta go home a long time ago. Back to New York. I just," Josh stammered. "You're gonna be a real fine doctor."

Britta wanted to hug him. Her heart was pounding, her cheeks flushed. Instead she directed him to hold on to the bars and try moving his left leg, which seemed to be strongest. She patiently waited, not saying anymore.

Josh took a deep breath, his jaw muscles clenching with concentration. He was perspiring with effort. He wanted so badly to move his leg, not only for himself but for Britta as well. Out of the blue, he thought of his brother Joe. *Lord, help me, Jesus.*

Ten minutes went by, Britta watching intently for the least movement. Then it happened. His left foot slid forward several inches! "Oh Josh! You did it!" In the most unprofessional way, she burst into tears.

"C'mere," he said. She was only a foot away to begin with, but he pulled her to his side, and with a bar between them, hugged her close. He kissed the top of her sweet-smelling hair. Britta melted into him. That's when Jack walked in.

Quickly Britta and Josh straightened, Britta rushing to explain. "We were just celebrating! He moved his foot Jack! Josh moved his foot!" She started to cry again.

With a huge smile on his face, Jack simply said, "I'll fetch the milk and cookies."

# Chapter 25

On their wedding night, Charles and Eula Mae Alexander had gone by horse and buggy to the other end of town, the Witherspoon house. The kitchen restoration was complete and new wallpaper had been hung in the parlor, the smell of smoke almost completely gone. "Witherspoon's Furniture Shop" next to the house, was being transformed to "Alexander Saddles." Joe and Uncle Charlie were in the process of transporting Charlie's tools, leather supplies, saddle stands, and all manner of paraphernalia, from the ranch.

On Friday morning, Betsy, Britta, Hilly, and Sloan had gone down to help Eula Mae with the house. They did a thorough spring cleaning, washed the windows, and waxed the oak floors. Joe and Jack would come later and bring Josh, after they helped with his therapy.

Joe could hardly believe his eyes. "I'm impressed, Uncle Charlie! Your new saddlemakin' shop is really shapin' up—orderly." Joe looked around the cabin-like shop. A fire crackled in the small stove, warming the place nicely. Windows on the east side gave good light over the workbench and wall pegs displayed various leathers. Saddle stands were placed strategically, some supporting half-built saddles.

"I'm glad yer here, Joe. Somethin' disturbin' happened this mornin'." Charlie motioned him over to one of the saddles he was working on. Without saying any more, he turned it so Joe could see the cantle. Understanding hit Joe suddenly, bringing with it long-buried anger. The cantle was covered in snakeskin. Diamondback. "Where's the lowdown polecat headed to, Charlie? When's he comin' back?" Joe's face was red with fury.

"I told him it'd take me till tomorrow noon to replace these stirrup straps. Both nearly worn through. What'll we do, Joe?" The two discussed ideas while Charlie worked on the outlaw's saddle. One thing was decided for sure: they wouldn't tell the women.

About midafternoon, after Eula Mae's delightful lunch, Sloan, Hilly, and the girls headed back to the boardinghouse. There was still work to be done. Next week, however, Sloan's load would lighten significantly. Juanita Gomez would take over the kitchen, three days a week.

On the buggy ride home, Betsy and Britta got to talking about Eula Mae. "She is remarkable," Britta commented. "She looks more like New York than Baker City, always dressed in the finest."

They got the giggles thinking about her many outfits, all with matching hats and how no one had ever seen her less than coordinated, tip to toe. "Even on this workday! And look at *us*." Betsy burst out laughing. Both girls wore their hair in loosely braided pigtails, strands sticking out in all directions. Britta had worn one of Betsy's faded calicos. Both had donned their old horse-riding coats and pulled on work boots. They looked like two Betsys.

All four women were laughing enthusiastically when they burst through the back door, their arms loaded with bundles from the mercantile. The four halted abruptly. Britta gasped. She couldn't believe her eyes. To her shock and alarm, there at the kitchen table sat Mother and Father: the Lundgrens.

———

Late afternoon, Joe stopped by the sheriff's office for a visit with Sheriff Stevens. The saddle was evidence enough that it's owner had been in on the bank robbery. The bank robbery that made his brother an invalid. It had been six months since that fateful day. The scene of Josh lying in a pool of blood had never left Joe's mind, especially when he passed by the jail, knowing that reprobate bank robber was still in there. The circuit judge would schedule a hearing when there were more cases for trial. Evidently the judge had bigger fish to fry.

Joe had planned to ask Sheriff Stevens to step out on the porch, to discuss the strategy he and Charlie had come up with, to keep it quiet.

Sheriff Stevens was not at his desk. The place seemed deserted. "Sheriff?" Joe called out. A muffled sound came from the storage closet. Joe drew his gun and quickly opened the closet door. There, bound and gagged, sat the sheriff, dried blood on his face. "What in the world?" Joe quickly ripped off the dirty neckerchief and cut the rope that bound Sheriff Stevens.

The sheriff moaned and blinked, squinting against the light. He didn't know how long he'd been in that closet, but guessed overnight. "Check the cell, Joe. I got a feelin' whoever knocked me out, freed our prisoner. Ain't been a sound comin' from that direction."

Joe hurried down the hall to find the cell door open. Instead of an empty cell, a body lay crumpled on the floor. Clem Holiday was dead as a doornail, shot point-blank.

The next day, noon came and went, but nobody picked up the saddle. "He probably had to skedaddle out of town bareback, after shootin' that Holiday bum." Charlie looked up to see Eula Mae come through the door with coffee and cookies for the men.

"Mr. Holiday has been shot?" she asked with a look of concern. Charlie explained the whole thing as delicately as possible. Joe held back from saying how he felt about it. "Well," Eula Mae began, "he's in a better place." She saw the best in everything.

Joe mumbled, "A *hotter* place in his case. The no-account."

"Oh, Mr. Holiday repented and turned to the Lord a few weeks back," Eula Mae announced with a smile. "He loved hearing me read the Bible. 'Book of hope,' he called it."

Joe was stunned and Uncle Charlie flabbergasted. "I done married me an angel," he said, smiling at his beautiful wife.

No one knew, except the pastor of Baker Baptist, that Eula Mae had been visiting Clem Holiday once a week—all these months. "Clem loved Sloan's huckleberry pie!" she exclaimed.

When Charlie went out to his shop early next morning, to get a fire going, he stopped dead in his tracks. A window on the east wall had been shattered, glass all over his workbench. The diamondback saddle—gone.

He didn't tell his wife, but later that day over afternoon tea (a new tradition for Charlie) he shared his thoughts. "Eula Mae, darlin', I think we need to expand our family." Eula Mae's eyes opened wide. She clasped a hand over her mouth, her cheeks turning pink.

Charlie went on, "I'm gonna have Joe bring the dogs ta town. Sarge and Sarge. Be a good idear for 'em to keep watch over the place."

"Oh my!" she exclaimed, clapping her hands together. "How lovely."

# Chapter 26

Dr. and Mrs. Lundgren had reserved the finest suites, such as they were, in the best hotel in Baker City, along with a room for their servant, Carter. "You brought Carter?" Britta was looking like Britta again that morning, as she met her parents for breakfast. She had dressed in a sophisticated suit and pulled her hair up into a smart twist.

"Well, of course, Britta. We need assistance on this journey. Grandmother and Grandfather are staying with the boys and we've hired temporary help for Rosa in the kitchen." She abruptly changed the subject. "Britta, we're not here for a holiday. We've come to take you home."

Britta picked at her food. She turned her attention toward her father. "I'm anxious for you to meet Josh, the young man I've been working with." She described the bank robbery in September, Josh taking a bullet. She explained the location and type of wound that caused his paralysis. Her father was keenly interested, asking numerous questions.

Alecia absently stirred her tea. "The point, dear," she shifted the focus back to Britta's going home, "we're scheduled to be on the train, leaving here in five days. Your father went to great lengths to have a surgeon from Philadelphia cover for him during our absence."

Britta, her enthusiasm unhampered, continued speaking to her father. "With physical therapy methods, that you taught me, Father, Josh has gone from being bed-ridden to standing at the bars. Just last week he moved his foot."

Dr. Lundgren understood. "I'd like to meet him."

"Britta, surely there is a local doctor that can take over. Besides, it's God who will decide if this young man walks again. Not you."

"Yes, Mother. I understand that." *But there's more, much more. I have—feelings for him.*

It was decided Britta and her father would walk to the boardinghouse, and Alecia would have Carter drive her later, just before dinner.

Josh was anxiously waiting when Britta walked in with Dr. Lundgren. Their sophisticated appearance reminded him where they had come from, New York. He took a deep breath and swallowed. He knew the Lundgrens had come to take their daughter home.

"Father, this is Josh Reed. Josh, my father, Edward Lundgren." Josh was sitting in the wheelchair, like he was ready to go out. The men shook hands. "Do you feel like taking a 'walk,' Josh?"

"Britta has shared your situation, Mr. Reed, and she's very optimistic for full recovery." Dr. Lundgren went on. "I'd like to see what you're working on, if now is a good time."

"Your daughter is amazin, sir. She's been truly devoted to helpin' me walk, an army sergeant in disguise." Josh chuckled, looking at Britta like she hung the moon. He wheeled his chair to the bars and pulled himself up, standing for a moment. Britta stood facing him, at the opposite end of the parallel bars. He released his hold, then looking right at her, grimacing slightly with effort, moved his left foot forward. He rested a moment. Then the right one, slowly inched forward until his feet were parallel.

Britta burst out in a huge smile. "Good, Josh!" She struggled not to cry. They continued looking at each other. Josh took a deep breath. Beads of perspiration glistened on his forehead. He did it again. Josh had set a record, two steps!

About that time, Doc Cartwright stopped by to check on his patient. The two doctors were introduced, everyone exuberant about Josh's progress. Britta was aware of the stark contrast in her father and Dr. Cartwright. Dr. Lundgren was impeccably dressed in his tailored cutaway coat, the steel gray complementing the graying at his temples. His white shirt, black brocade vest, and highly polished black shoes gave him an air of refinement. Doc Cartwright, on the other hand, looked like the average cowboy in Baker, from his hat to his boots, which were caked in mud. "I just been makin' my rounds in the rural areas," he explained. "Helped Ben Hadley pull a calf while I was out there," he said, apologizing for the mud tracked in.

Both doctors agreed Britta was on the right track with Josh. The three discussed some additional thoughts on firing up his leg muscles, bringing them back to life. "In my opinion," Doc said, "another few weeks of workin' on the bars, then maybe build strength sitting to standing, gradually depending less on the upper body."

"I concur," Dr. Lundgren said. *Britta must stay and see this through. If I can only convince her mother.*

Before Doc Cartwright left, he invited Dr. Lundgren to visit the construction site of the new Baker City Hospital.

———

Joe and Betsy finally had some time together—alone. She had gone out with him and Uncle Charlie for a final cleaning of the ranch house. Charlie had left to go back home early afternoon, with the last wagonload, leaving Joe and Betsy to clean house. They were leisurely riding their horses back to town, on an uncommonly warm March day. "We've made our plans, Bets, but I've gotta talk to your mother. I haven't wanted to add to her anxiety with Britta here and all."

"And I'm so happy Britta's still here, but yes. We better tell Mama." She looked at her future husband lovingly. "Soon as we have her blessin', we can tell everybody!" They discussed their plans for the wedding. "It's a long shot that Britta will still be here in June. I've been prayin' about it though. And prayin' about her and Josh."

"Josh?" Joe looked perplexed.

"Don't tell me ya haven't noticed! The way they look at each other? Things are changin' with 'em, Joe. It's gone from doctor and patient, to somethin deeper. I keep thinkin' she's gonna tell me."

Joe laughed. "Now that's a wonder! I feel bad for both of 'em, if it's true. Josh is hopeful but don't know if he's ever gonna be back to his old self. Probably scared to make a declaration toward Britta. If it's true."

"And Britta is surely torn. After all, her whole life she's been determined on bein' a doctor. Goin' to medical school and all."

Joe motioned to a big cottonwood, just off the trail. They would rest a spell, while the horses drank from a lazy stream beyond the tree. "I'm gonna pray for 'em too," Joe said seriously as he considered Betsy's pretty face. Then he broke out in a big smile. "Wouldn't that be somethin'? Twins married ta twins?"

"Oh, that has definitely crossed my mind Joey." She smiled up at him and he pulled her into his arms, relishing the moment before he kissed her sweet lips deeply, his heart full of love.

# Chapter 27

It was the day before their scheduled departure. Alecia had come over to the boardinghouse to help Britta pack. Edward had not made much headway convincing his wife to let the girl stay. When they entered the kitchen, Sloan graciously received them. "Please sit down for a moment." She poured coffee and set cream and sugar on the table. This wouldn't be easy.

"We don't have much time, Sloan dear. We need to get Britta's and Hilly's trunks to the hotel tonight. They will be picked up for delivery to the station early in the morning."

Edward spoke up. "It's fine, Alecia. You and Sloan haven't had much time together." He had felt a strain between them over the time of their visit.

Sloan took a sip of coffee. "It's been wonderful having Britta here. She's a beautiful and brilliant girl. She and Betsy have become close, not only as sisters, but friends. I am so grateful that you permitted her to come. Thank you for that."

Alecia opened her mouth to say something, but Sloan continued. "I'm so proud of her for dedicating long days to helpin' Josh. She has done wonders with her therapy treatments." Sloan kept talking. "Josh and Joe are the finest young men I've ever known. Watchin' them care for each other made me realize how important it was for

Britta and Betsy to be reunited. There's somethin' unique about twins."

"And I'm sure, Sloan, that Dr. Cartwright can continue the therapy. He's bound to be more qualified. Britta's not even a doctor. She's been gone too long as it is."

Sloan looked down in her cup. "There's more." She took a deep breath. "Your daughter," she looked at both parents, wanting them to know she fully understood Lundgren's were Britta's legal parents. "Britta has fallen in love with Josh."

Alecia's mouth flew open, her hand knocking over the cup. "What are you saying? Sloan, you know nothing of my daughter's feelings. But I know what you're doing. Don't interfere. We are taking her home and that is final!" Alecia's nerves were shot. She struggled against tears.

Edward had been drinking his coffee, sitting back letting the women converse. He sat forward. "How do you know that Britta is in love with Josh?"

"She told me last night," said Sloan. "Britta's heart is breaking. She doesn't want to leave, but knows it's expected."

Edward spoke again. "And Josh? Do you know how he feels toward Britta?"

Sloan couldn't help herself. She chuckled. "All of us can see he's crazy about her. I've been prayin' about it. Truly I have. And I'm askin' you to please consider letting her stay. At least another month or two. See what God has in mind. She doesn't start school until September. I'm just asking you. Please let Britta stay."

Edward looked at his wife tenderly. "Sweetheart, there's really no reason—"

She cut him off. "No! Absolutely not." Alecia stormed from the room, leaving through the front door, slamming it shut behind her.

Late that afternoon, Britta knocked softly on Josh's open door. It would be their last "session." "Feel like taking a walk?" She tried sounding normal, composed, medical.

Josh smiled from where he sat on the edge of the bed. He'd been waiting for her all day.

*Help me, Lord. Help me stay strong.* Britta walked to the far end of the parallel bars as Josh made his way in the wheelchair.

When finally, he had pulled himself up, standing for a minute, he began the hard work of moving his feet. The left foot seemed more cooperative, the right still struggled, sliding forward.

"Good, Josh!" Britta's heart was racing. She clenched her jaw to hold back tears. "Go ahead. Try it again," she said, hoping not to sound like her heart was breaking.

His brown eyes held her blue ones, bright with unshed tears. He took another step.

Britta took a step toward him. Neither spoke words, but meaning was conveyed between them.

Perspiring now, Josh took another step. Britta did too. They stood close, looking at each other.

With urgency, Josh pulled her into his strong arms. "Don't go, Britta. Please don't go." He spoke into her hair.

Britta collapsed against him, breaking down and crying into his chest. "You don't need me anymore Josh," she sobbed.

They clung to each other, letting go their true feelings.

"I love you, Britta. I want to spend my life with you. I picture us buildin' a house in the country, filling the yard with kids. It's the dream that keeps me goin'. Please don't leave." Moisture escaped his own eyes.

Britta looked up, her face wet with tears. She felt so much love for this man. Nothing else mattered. She looked at him, beseeching. "Well then, can we have a dog?"

He smiled, taking her face in his hands. "Was that a yes?"

"Was that a proposal?"

He kissed her passionately then, and Britta didn't hesitate. She kissed back with longing.

Jack had the good sense to peek through the crack in the door, before charging in. He stepped backward, putting a finger to his lips. "She's stayin'," he whispered to Lefty. Lefty ran over to the stove. Putting a finger to his lips, he whispered, "Madre, she's stayin'!"

Sloan was sitting on the front porch with Joe and Betsy, discussing wedding plans. Mrs. Bush, who rarely knew what was going on, poked her head out the door. "She's a stayin'!"

———

The good-byes at the train station were mixed with happiness and tears. Britta clung to Hilly, missing her already. "I been watchin' ya grow up, baby. All these years. But here in Oregon, you truly grew up. I love ya, baby. I'll miss ya terrible. But I'm comin' back, girl. Yes, sireee. I be back!"

Alecia looked pale but resigned. Sloan wrapped her in a warm hug. "You haven't lost your daughter, Alecia. It's the way of things. Please come for the wedding—she wants that. She wants her father to walk her down the aisle. Please come. I love you, sister."

Edward wrapped his daughter in a warm hug. "Mother will be all right, dear," he said reassuringly. "We gave you to God the day we adopted you. We must trust him with your life, sweetheart. She will see that eventually."

There was only Britta and her mother who had not yet said good-bye. They stood, awkwardly looking at each other. Alecia squeezed her eyes shut, holding back tears. "I love you, Mama." It was the first-time Britta had ever said, "Mama." There was something warm, personal about it. Alecia hugged her daughter tight. "I love you too, Britta." She turned toward the train.

"Oh, I forgot!" Britta hurried to catch her. "Here's a present for the boys. It's actually from Jack." She handed her mother the package wrapped in butcher paper. "It's his steer ropin' rope."

At last they boarded the train that would eventually take her parents, Carter and Hilly, back to New York. Without Britta. The last thing she heard as the family disappeared was Hilly's voice. "Now what them boys gonna do with a ropin' rope? They probably kill each other."

———

Everyone was waiting at the kitchen table when Sloan walked in with Betsy, Joe, and Britta. There sat Uncle Charlie and Eula Mae, Juanita, Lefty, and Jack. Josh from his wheelchair, motioned Britta over, taking her hand in his.

Joe and Betsy pulled up to the table, Juanita passed the coffeepot. Sloan remained standing, smiling at each one—her heart full. *Thank you, Lord, for a most wonderful family.*

"I'd like to make an announcement," she said sweetly. Imitating Eula Mae, she cleared her throat. "Your presence is requested at noon, on the first Sunday in June, at Baker Baptist Church. There will be," she began, happy tears escaping, "a double, double wedding!" Everyone knew exactly who she meant without saying their names. A loud cheer went up, each one laughing or crying, shouting out congratulations jumping up to hug the happy couples.

Like the end of a fairy tale, the Reed brothers, two young men who rode into town that long-ago September day, with no plans to stay, had discovered the loves of their lives. "Grandmother was right," said Jack. "God *does* work in mysterious ways."

Juanita roughed up his hair lovingly. "Si!" she agreed. "And tonight, we have tamales!"

# Chapter 28

For the next three months, everyone would work on some aspect of the June weddings. Sloan and the girls, with Eula Mae's expertise, cut out, fitted, and stitched their wedding gowns. Betsy and Britta had chosen slightly different patterns using the same fabric, which had been ordered from Portland.

Joe and Uncle Charlie labored at the ranch, building a small log house on the back meadow. Extra help, in the form of Jack, Lefty, and even Josh, worked on the weekends, equally enthused for Joe and Betsy's new home.

Sloan had decreed that Josh and Britta would live in the main house, at least for summer months. Stair rails would be added out front and other modifications inside, to accommodate Josh. The whole family hoped and prayed by the June wedding, that Josh would be much improved.

Before Dr. Lundgren had left town, he and Britta, at Doc Cartwright's invitation, had visited the new hospital. Even though it was a far cry from Providence Hospital in New York City, father and daughter were quite impressed. Britta loved that despite the "modern" facility, it had a homey feel. The walls of each ward were painted in pale shades of blue and sage green, and featured print curtains — compliments of the women of the local churches.

They had been standing in a large unfinished space on the backside of the building. Tall windows looked out on undeveloped land, leading to the forest, a peaceful view. "Our plans for this space," said Doc Cartwright, "is for a rehabilitation unit." He excitedly continued describing features he hoped to include. "Eventually, we plan to appoint a rehab facilitator." He looked straight at Britta and smiled.

———

Josh had made a sudden turn in progress, walking the full length of the parallel bars. He could make it all the way to the end, where the "most beautiful girl in the world" would be patiently waiting, her lips puckered. His hope and determination had soared since the day she had said yes! The fact that they were so in love, however, was a bit of a distraction. On a morning in April, when Josh lingered over his "reward" of a kiss at the end of the walk, Britta said, "All right, Josh. Back to work." In her most professional voice, she commanded him to turn around and walk the other way.

"Oh c'mon, Britta. Don't be so hard on a guy!" he was teasing, but also felt close to exhaustion. He would try though. For her, he would try.

On May 1, Britta had the bars removed altogether. Josh wasn't ready for a foot race, but he could make his way across the room, unaided. *Praise you, Lord.*

———

Meanwhile, back in Thatcher Springs, Kate burst in through the front door of the inn, waving a letter. "It's from the boys!" Even though they were turning twenty-two in July, they would always be her "boys." She had held off opening the letter until she could share it with Max, who was helping Silas do repairs in the dining room. Millie rushed in from the kitchen.

"Open it, Kate!" Millie said bursting with excitement. "I hope they're still comin'!" A shadow of concern was in her eyes.

Kate ripped it open, while the other three watched her every move. She scanned the first paragraph before reading aloud. The huge smile on her face, crumpled. She suddenly looked like she'd seen a ghost. With a gasp, she clamped a hand over her mouth and burst into tears. "I can't believe it!" She sobbed. The unread letter fell on the floor as Max leaped to her side.

"What?" He feared the worst.

"Are twinners all right? Did somebody die?" Millie had turned pale at Kate's reaction.

"Tell us, Kate." Silas took a deep breath, preparing for the terrible news.

Kate could barely speak through her sobbing. "They," she tried again. "They, they—they got—married!" She collapsed into Max's embrace. Silas pulled Millie into his arms. Both women now full out bawling. Silas, consoling Millie, looked up at Max, consoling Kate. Max smiled a devious smile and winked. Silas smiled back, reading Max's mind. "Will wonders never cease."

———

Though simple, it had been the most extraordinary wedding the town had ever witnessed. Britta's parents, her two brothers, Hilly, and Carter had come, to Britta's joy. Of course, the "immediate family," the congregation, Mrs. Bush, and all her boarders had attended; in fact, most of Baker City was at that wedding. Lefty's padre rode into town to join his wife and son for the occasion. By the time the ceremony began, there had been standing room only at Baker Baptist.

Joshua and Joseph Reed *both* stood tall, handsome, and identical. They wore dark western-cut suits and neckerchiefs, a tradition of Thatcher Springs. Their boots were shiny as their faces, smiling with happiness.

Betsy came down the aisle first, on the arm of Uncle Charlie. Though no one could tell the grooms apart, Betsy looked right at

Joe, meaning passed between them. She had chosen to wear her hair long, blonde curls cascading down her back. It was Joe's favorite way. Her gown was simple, tiny buttons at the high collar, long sleeves, and fitted to her tiny waist. The only color, a pale blue satin sash, matching Joe's neckerchief. Three ruffles at the hem, flounced with every step.

Britta followed, on her father's arm. Dr. Lundgren looked at her lovingly as they walked down the aisle. When she gazed at Josh, unbidden tears spilled down her cheeks. She loved him. She would love him if he had never left his wheelchair. "You are so courageous," she whispered.

Her gown was similar to Betsy's. The skirt matched exactly with three tiers of ruffles at the hem, the sleeves long, and the blue satin sash. She had chosen a scooped neckline, knowing it would make her mother happy to wear the single strand pearl choker that Alecia had worn when she married Edward. Her hair was also styled to her mother's liking, swooped up into an elegant chignon. The brides carried wild yellow roses that not only had survived Jack's roping attempts, but had come back twofold.

The couples were attended by Eula Mae on the bride's side and Jack on the groom's. Eula Mae was dressed in a soft blue velvet ensemble, of course, with a matching hat, tipped fashionably to one side. Jack looked like a shorter version of the two grooms, dressed exactly like them. Josh had often referred to the three of them as triplets anyway.

Sloan sat with Alecia and Edward in the front pew. All she could do was praise God. She was on cloud nine, happy for her daughters, her beautiful twin girls. Could it be anything short of a miracle? *Oh, Jonathon, how I wish you were here today.* After all these years since her husband's death, she had missed him every single day. Alecia reached across Edward and took Sloan's hand.

---

"Did somebody die?" Grace walked in and immediately went to her mother's side. "Mother? What is it?" Millie was still bawling, out of control.

Silas looked at Grace. "Somethin' like that. Josh and Joey got hitched. They's married men now." Then he whispered over the top of Millie's head, "Millie and Kate's a little put out they didn't know about it, missed the whole shebang. They'll get over it."

Millie pounded his chest. "I will *not* get over it!" she exclaimed through her tears.

Grace stifled a giggle.

Just then, Simone and Margot walked in. They stopped in their tracks. "What is it, Grace?" Simone whispered.

"Josh and Joe got married!" Grace whispered back.

Kate blew her nose, recovering a bit. An idea taking shape. "Millie?"

Millie sniffed and wiped her eyes. "I just can't believe it."

"Millie," Kate continued, "what if we plan a wedding reception at the family reunion?"

Millie recovered rather quickly at the idea. "Kate! That's a fine idea. We could order a wedding cake and—well, we must get word that the wives bring their wedding gowns, whoever they are."

"Says here they're twins," declared Max. He had sat down to read the letter.

"Well, we *know* that. Honestly, Max." Kate thought her husband had gone daffy.

"The wives. Says here the wives are twins too. Identical. Betsy—that's Joe's. And Britta, that one is Josh's wife."

Millie marched over to Josh. "Let me see that." She grabbed the letter out of his hand like he had read it wrong. A smile escaped through her tears. She looked over at Kate. "Well, bless Pat."

———

Sloan was so thankful the day had turned out sunny and beautiful. One never knew in eastern Oregon. The wedding had been planned in conjunction with the first Sunday potluck and the women of the church had outdone themselves to create an enormous spread featuring their best recipes. To Alecia's dismay, the potluck doubled as a wedding reception for the happy couples. She had always pictured an elaborate affair, in their third-floor ballroom. Nonetheless, Britta looked so happy. All four, in seventh heaven.

As things were wrapping up, Josh and Joe finally had a chance to congratulate each other. They hugged the way men do, giving each other a hearty slap on the back. "Can you believe we just became married men?" Joe laughed. "Millie and Kate are gonna kill us!" They both laughed heartily, then Joe turned serious. "I am so proud of you, brother. Look at you! No one would guess." He choked up and couldn't finish the sentence.

"I wouldn't have made it without you, Joey. Thank you for stickin' with me. Doin' the work for both of us." Understanding passed between them.

Joe chuckled. "Remember that story Kate used to tell us? The one where the cowboy got bucked off his horse and was lame until the princess kissed him?"

"Think of it often," Josh said, smiling. "That's our story now Joe. Just like the happy ending to a fairy tale."

"Except this one's real, Josh. And it's just the happy beginning."

*Part 3*

# MILLIE

*Blest be the tie that binds, our hearts in one accord.*
—*John Fawcett, 1782*

# Chapter 29

"All aboard!" the conductor shouted, and the train lurched to a start. At last, the Thatcher Springs family was off to the Oregon coast.

Millie was laughing like a schoolgirl. "Can ya believe it, Silas? We're really goin'. It's really gonna happen!"

Silas seemed a bit on edge. "Honey did ya member my shavin' blade?"

"Yes, sweetheart. I got it."

"What about my blue shirt?"

"It's in the trunk." Millie would *never* forget his favorite shirt, the one she had made for their wedding,

Just as Millie was beginning to unwind, captivated by the view zooming by, Silas thought of something else. "Did ya remember ta tell Sherriff Buckingham what ta do if the stove starts smokin'?"

"Yes, Silas, now try to relax. I promise everything is taken care of. I double-checked all my lists, just before we left." She changed the subject. "Want a blanket, sweetheart? Maybe take a nap," she suggested.

Silas couldn't settle down. He brought up another six things that she might have forgotten.

"Silas," she began, "we have everything we need. Sherriff Buckingham is fully aware of every detail of Thatcher Springs. He and his wife and two sons are on duty and his posse will arrive this evening. Now please, honey, quit worryin'. Nothin' can go wrong!"

———

"Mother, have you seen Sammy?" Grace inquired calmly.

"No, dear, but he must be with the other boys. Maybe in the observation car?" Millie felt a flutter of unease in her chest. She decided to leave her seat to do her own search. Silas, the poor man, had finally fallen asleep. They had stopped for a meal at the depot in southwestern Utah and now were chugging along in Nevada. The chicken dinner had been pretty good—considering—and Silas seemed to calm down after that.

By that time, the rest of the family had begun searching for Sammy. Millie went car to car, from one end of the train to the other. "Samuel? Sammy!" She described him to curious passengers. "He's about this tall, with dark hair and blue eyes. Oh dear. Sammy!" With each car, she became more upset and started crying. Then she would get angry. "If you are hidin', Samuel, it's not funny. You are in big trouble if you are hidin'!" And then she would start crying again with worry.

———

Sammy loved to climb trees. Whenever his family went on picnics or fishing, it always included tree climbing. Even his mother, Grace, climbed with Sam and the boys. After dinner at the Utah depot, Sammy had wandered outside, absentmindedly looking for obsidian or any other nice rocks for his collection. Out back some ways, he spotted a fine tall tree and trotted out to climb it.

In no time, he was high above the depot. He could see miles of tracks in both directions. From the top of that tree, he could see little black spots on the meadows, cows grazing. From the top of that tree, Sammy spotted a coyote loping along the fence line and a doe with her fawn, drinking from a stream. It was from the top of that tree that Sammy watched the back end of the train he was supposed to be on pull out of the station, heading west. "Oh oh."

Not all that long ago the depot was teaming with activity. Now it was nearly deserted. A hobo sat on the lone bench outside. He was filthy dirty, his clothes so old that the patches had patches. Sammy went over and sat by him. "You get left behind too?" he asked the man.

The old guy answered, "Yeah," with a bit of sarcasm, "'bout fifty years ago."

"What's yer name?"

The man hesitated, still looking straight ahead. Finally said, "Merle."

"You hungry, Merle?"

"What if I was? Ain't got no coins."

Sammy sat there thinking. "Be right back, Merle."

Fifteen minutes later, the boy returned dragging a broom, three times his size and carrying a dustpan. "If we sweep this whole platform," he spread his arm wide, "the ticket man will give us two bits. Enough for a chicken dinner."

Merle seemed to see Sammy for the first time. The little squirt had gone and got him a job. He was stiff as a board and feeling weak, but for a meal, he could do it. The grimy hobo and six-year-old Indian boy with blue eyes worked together, Merle sweeping and Sammy holding the dustpan.

It took a good hour, but they finally completed the task and the ticket man honored his promise to pay. Since the dining room was technically closed, the ticket man spoke with the cook. "I'm not specially strong on feedin' hobos but he did earn it. And the kid, missin' the train and all. Just give 'em whatever ya can, Slim."

Leftover fried chicken, and spuds with gravy looked like a feast to Merle. They had been served only one plate, but Slim had added an extra piece of chicken.

Merle was ready to dive in, then looked across the table at Sammy. "Go ahead and pick the piece ya want."

Sammy took a leg and bowed his head. "Thank you, Lord, for this chicken leg. Amen."

After dinner, the ticket man called Sammy over to the counter. "We wired ahead to Elko. That's where your family be stoppin' next. The afternoon westbound be comin' through at four o'clock tomorrow. You get on it and when the conductor comes around for your ticket, you say, 'It's on the other end.' Got it?" He hadn't mentioned Merle.

"Yes, sir."

"As far as where yer gonna sleep tonight? Well, guess you'll just have ta figure it out yerself."

Sammy and Merle were back to sitting on the bench, chatting. Mostly little Sam doing the chatting. It was turning dusk. "Be right back, Uncle Merle."

The boy returned after a bit. "I think I figured it out."

"Figured what out?"

"Where we gonna sleep tonight."

Merle expected to sleep right there on the bench, but he followed Sammy inside. The place was empty, except for the ticket man who worked at his desk by lamplight. Beyond the ticket counter, across from the dining room, there were several polished wood doors with frosted glass on the upper half. Gold lettering described the contents behind each door. "Right here. See, Uncle Merle? This is where we're s'posed ta sleep— 'Lost and Found'."

———

Millie was inconsolable. "Why did I ever think this was gonna work? I knew everything would go wrong."

It was Silas now calming his wife, tying to reassure her everything would be fine. "Darlin', it's just a little hiccup. Sammy's gonna be okay. You'll see." He hoped he was right.

When the train screeched to a halt at the Elko Station, in Nevada, the family disembarked like a herd, and rushed inside. A wire had come which simply said, "WEAVER ON WESTBOUND TOMORROW. STOP."

The train departed Elko with everyone's luggage and trunks still onboard. Sammy's entire Thatcher Springs family stayed behind to wait for him. By the time tickets were reissued for the next day and rooms arranged at the Elko Hotel for everyone to spend the night, Millie was only partly relieved. "Oh, my poor baby. Wonder where he'll sleep tonight? What if he's hungry? What if he's scared?"

The boy's father, Samuel, put an arm around her. "Sammy's gonna be fine, Miss Millie. Don't fret so."

"But Sam," she cried, "he's so little!"

"Yes, ees true. He's leetle. But don't forget, Miss Millie, Sammy leetle *Indian*. He'll figure it out."

When the train had left Utah the following day, Sammy insisted Merle come too. After a while the conductor came through collecting tickets. Remembering what the ticket man had told him, Sammy said, "My ticket is at the other end."

The conductor looked at Merle with disgust. "What about *you,* bub?" Merle squirmed in his seat.

"His ticket is at the other end too." Sammy said with confidence. He knew without a doubt his family would pay Merle's faire. He knew without a doubt, they would be kind and accepting to the dirty, grimy hobo with patches on his patches.

———

By the time they had arrived in San Francisco, everyone was recovered from the Sammy episode, had settled into enjoying the journey again. Their rooms at the Grand Hotel would be ready at four o'clock, giving them a good hour wait. The concierge suggested they make themselves comfortable in the library, where tea would be served. Millie and Silas, compliments of Cody, had stayed there once before, but still marveled at the opulence. The rest of the family stood in awe, unable to move from the lobby. Kate and Grace,

Simone and Margot were giddy with excitement. The children thought they must be in a castle and wanted to touch everything.

Max and Silas offered to take "Uncle Merle" to the nearest bathhouse for a bath and shave, and while he was there, they would go down the street to the Emporium, as the bellhop had directed, to buy Merle a new suit of clothes.

"Tea" in the library was a whole lot more than tea. There were fancy little sandwiches and teacakes, cookies and lemonade made with California lemons. Everyone began to relax, recounting the last few days on the train. When the conversation turned to Sammy, Kate asked the boy about Merle. "Do you know anything about 'Uncle Merle'?"

Sammy stuffed one more small cake into his mouth, thinking. "Well, he musta fought in the war. He was proud to wear the Union Blue, and the last one standing on that hill, so he covered up the dead." Sammy had to think a minute. "Oh, and he left his girl in Kentucky and, let's see. He drove a thousand cows to Canada! And he shot a man in Texas." Sammy left out the part where Merle got drunk first.

Everyone was captivated. His mother, Grace, asked, "Did he tell you all that?"

"He sung it. There was a guitar in the 'Lost and Found' room, where we slept. Uncle Merle sang about his whole life. I fell asleep after he shot the man in Texas, so that's all I know."

# Chapter 30

Sherriff Buckingham and his wife, Martha, thought they'd hit the jackpot, landing the job in Thatcher Springs. They had the whole inn to themselves, which Millie had made sure was well stocked. In fact, they had the whole *town* to themselves. Buck smiled, "This here's a real paid vacation, Martha, a kinda second honeymoon." He winked.

"Well, Bucky, remember we have a big obligation here, tendin' the animals and keepin' the town safe." Martha was the responsible type. "But I confess it'll be pleasurable livin' in this nice place, cookin' on a fine cook-stove. Between the pantry and the cooler, we're gonna be eatin' real good. And the boys are already havin' a grand time!"

The Buckinghams had brought their two youngest of five boys, the other three stayed back to take care of the farm and rotate sitting in the sheriff's office in town. Their pa had deputized all three, ranging in age from seventeen to twenty-two. "They'll be fine," he assured Martha. "Nothin much happens in Clearwater, Wyoming. I coulda left Birdie Fletcher in charge!" He busted up laughing at his own joke. Birdie was ninety-four.

"The posse we got comin' should be showin up fore dark, anytime now. Course it'll be extra mouths ta feed, but them men'll be doin' the dirty work of night duty. We won't have a thing ta worry about. They's real qualified too. Come on good recommendation from the sheriff in Boise."

Just as Martha called the boys in for supper from the back porch, the dogs started barking out front. Sure enough, a wagon pulled up with three individuals seated on the bench, a team of two horses pulling them. "Here comes our posse, Martha!" Buck shouted, and all four ran out front to greet them.

Buck stopped dead in his tracks. "What in tarnation?" He pulled off his hat and squinted up at the three to get a better look. "They's women!" he said, mostly to himself. "Uh, greetin's and salutations, ladies. What can we do fer ya?"

The one closest to him spoke up. "You must be Sherriff Buckingham. Glad ta meet ya, sir. I'm Dellmira Jacobs." She turned to the one next to her. "And this is Louella Jacobs, and that one, our sister-in-law, Hallie Jacobs." The three ladies smiled their hellos.

"Well, the thing is, ladies, this here town is closed for a month." Buck was feeling queasy in his gut. "My family here and me, we're just caretakin' the place."

"Oh yes, I know," said Dellmira." We've come for the job. Us three." They all smiled and nodded. "We're your posse, sir."

"Uh, there must be some mistake."

Dellmira cut him off. "Well, ya see, sir, it was s'pposed ta be our two husbands and their brother, but somethin urgent came up. Some of our relatives were desperate for drovers to ride herd on a big ol' cattle drive. Last minute thing—couldn't be helped. But don't you worry none. We're qualified."

Buck was pinching the bridge of his nose, thinking what to do, when Martha stepped forward. She and the boys had hung back until they knew what was going on. "You girls must be worn out. Let's all go inside. We were about to sit down for supper and there's plenty." Martha seemed extra excited over this development.

Just then a squeaking sound came from the wagon, followed by a full-out wail. "Oh dear!" Dellmira exclaimed as she jumped down from the buckboard. "It's time ta feed the baby!"

———

Millie's heart was beating with anticipation. Three coaches had been arranged to transport the Thatcher Springs family, along with Ike and Esther Penrose, to the Inn at Seaside from the train station in Portland. They would settle in this evening, get their bearings, and the next day, the Baker folks would pull in and hopefully Cody and Lila. Gus and Pearl were scheduled to arrive the day after. With any luck, Kate's other sisters would arrive then too. It was a dream come true. All those she loved would be reunited on the Oregon coast.

The Inn at Seaside was a stately old building, rather plain from the outer appearance, but when Millie and Silas walked in ahead of the others, Millie was overcome. The entry hall alone was massive and looked straight out to the ocean through tall windows, opposite the entrance. The walls were faced in two shades of cream, wide-stripe wallpaper, with mahogany sideboards opposite each other. Large beveled glass mirrors hung above each one, reflecting the ocean. The polished oak floor featured an Oriental rug in shades of soft rose and teal blue.

An archway to their left opened to the gathering room, a huge space with elegant but cozy sofas and chairs arranged for conversation. The brocade wallpaper in shades of cream and white embellished the walls with elegance. The designer had carried out a picture-perfect mission, just as Millie had directed. Beautiful gilded frames hung on walls around the room between the polished wood posts. There was a mixture of shapes and sizes, the largest frame hanging above the stone fireplace. They were noticeably empty of any manner of artwork, just the frames. The west wall featured

French doors, opened to the sea, soft linen curtains billowing with ocean breezes.

Millie took Silas by the hand and walked to the windows. "Silas, darlin'," she said softly, "would ya say a prayer of thanks? And bless this place, honey. Bless it with gladness." As the rest of the family walked in, they stopped, gathered in the archway, and bowed their heads too.

———

It was quite an undertaking for the Baker City bunch, getting prepared for travel. So much had happened leading up to the wedding and then afterward. Joe, with everyone pitching in, had finished the cabin just in time. His bride had been completely surprised and overjoyed, laughing and crying at the sight of it. Joe and Betsy were so in love.

Josh was improving every day, getting around with just a cane, although crutches worked best when he was in a hurry. He and Britta had moved into the main house at McLemore Ranch, and though it was a far cry from the New York mansion Britta had grown up in, she was *home* with the man she loved.

Sloan had cut a deal with Pedro Gomez, to arrange for purchase and delivery of one hundred mother cows, now grazing on the meadow, a sight to behold. With the fence replaced or mended, and the grass lush and green, McLemore Ranch was back in business. She leaned on the gate gazing out over the meadow. "We did it, Jonathon. We got our ranch back." She let tears escape, a mixture of happiness and sorrow.

The two older Gomez brothers would camp at McLemore Ranch while the family was away, irrigate the fields, and tend the animals. Sloan would make sure they were well compensated. The fact that Juanita, their mother, would come out a couple days a week and cook for them, they declared was compensation enough. They had missed her tamales.

At last they were ready. The Reed brothers, their wives, Charlie and Eula Mae Alexander, Jack and his friend Lefty and Sloan. They headed to the train station with a wagonload of trunks. "Your grandmother must've brought all her fancy dresses," Josh whispered to Jack. "Course it didn't help Millie sendin' that wire. About the weddin'."

"What wire?" Jack asked.

"Oh, she sent a wire from the train stop in Utah, like it was a big emergency. Requested us ta bring all our weddin' duds, the bride dresses and all. Guess she's plannin' on reenactin' the weddin'."

Jack chuckled. "I can't wait to meet Miss Millie!"

———

After supper at the Inn of Thatcher Springs, Sherriff Buckingham went out back with his boys to help with evening chores. He'd had his fill of the kitchen full of women cooing over the baby and exchanging recipes. He breathed in the night air attempting to recover from the events of the day. "I'm between a rock and hard place," he muttered to the milk cow. "Just no choice in the matter, have ta work with what I got." That's what his pa always said anyway.

The next morning at breakfast, Sherriff Buck Buckingham took control. "At ten o'clock sharp, you three be back in this dinin' room, and ya better be lookin' like men. Me and the boys rustled up some duds from the bunkhouse, so y'all take this pile upstairs and figure it out." The three giggled. Martha was rocking Lucy, singing a lullaby in the background.

Buck continued. "And from now on, we're changin' yer names. Louella, yer gonna be Louie. Dellmira, Del. Ya got that?" He looked at little Hallie who stood proudly, all five feet of her. "Hallie," he rubbed his chin and let out a sigh. "You will be Hank. They all giggled again. "When I see you back here at ten sharp, ya better be lookin' like my posse."

A bit *after* ten sharp, the girls came downstairs, ready for their badges. They had piled their hair up under their hats and dressed in britches and shirts from the bunkhouse. Their own boots would have to do. "What in tarnation is this?" He scowled and yanked the hat off "Hank's" head. It was pure white felt and featured a crown of sparkling jewels.

"Hallie, er Hank, was Rodeo Queen of Homestead last year," Dellmira said proudly. "She rode in the Boise parade! Er he rode in the parade."

Buck rolled his eyes, his blood pressure elevating. "Go fetch that hat hangin' on the back porch," he ordered Martha, who was feeding the baby porridge. In the meantime, he went to the hearth and grabbed a piece of charred wood. "Ya'll need whiskers to be convincin'."

When Martha came back with the baby and the hat, Lucy took one look at her mama and then her two aunts and started to bawl. She could not be consoled. The "whiskers" Buck had smeared on their faces scared her to death. "Oh Bucky, that's not real good for their complexions, dear."

When Buck started to pin on the badges, a revelation hit him. "Hmm. This won't do," he muttered. "Maybe find some vests." He suggested Martha take the girls down to the leather shop and look for some loose-fitting vests.

"Oh goody," squealed Hallie. "We get ta go shoppin'!" The veins bulged out in Buck's neck.

When the women went out the door with keys to the leather shop, Martha handed off the baby to Buck. "See if you can get her to finish her porridge, dear."

# Chapter 31

Tom Carter was overjoyed with the kitchen, just as much as the others were thrilled with the whole place. It was spacious and well equipped with copper pots and pans, two commercial size cook-stoves, a large cooler, and two pantries. He would be cooking alongside the house chef and oversee a host of servers. Tom was grateful to be included in the family reunion and anxious to spend time with his younger brother Gus and wife Pearl, who happened to be Kate's sister. Her other two sisters, Ada and Liz, it was rumored, would be coming too.

Tom had set his guitar next to the piano in the gathering room, before taking his luggage upstairs. Each family had been assigned a private suite on the second and third floors, all with a veranda overlooking the Pacific Ocean.

That evening, the Thatcher Springs family—and Merle—congregated in the gathering room, after a delicious supper, where dessert would be served later. The women kicked off their shoes, relaxed and content. "I can't believe it." Millie chuckled. "Just listen to that big ol' ocean roar!" She closed her eyes, then suddenly they popped open, with an idea. "Let's go for a walk. On the beach!"

Kate burst out laughing. "Only you, Millie dear. Only you."

The children couldn't get out the door fast enough, and the men, though reluctant went along, all but Merle. It was a lovely sunset evening, white foamy waves iridescent as the tide receded.

The children laughed and ran and stumbled and laughed some more. The couples walked arm and arm, some holding hands. "Isn't this wonderful, Max?" Kate looked up at her husband in the golden glow of sunset. Their lives had been so busy with four children, a herd of cows, a bunch of horses, chickens all over the yard, hay fields to mow, and a garden to maintain. "It's," she hesitated, "kinda romantic." She got the giggles.

"What's so funny, Katy?" Max loved his wife more than ever.

"Don't think I'll ever get over it, Max, the way we—met." She giggled some more. "What were you thinkin' that day, when you saw me comin' at ya?"

Max laughed out loud. "Truth is, I was thinkin' my life was over! Little did I know, it was. The life I had known." Max and Kate had slowed, walking behind the others. He stopped and pulled her into his arms. They kissed like newlyweds.

As the family brushed the sand from their feet and walked back up the long stairs to the inn, they heard soft music coming from the open French doors. It was Merle strumming the guitar, singing like he was in another world. His voice was deep and rich, though years of whiskey and tobacco had given it a raspy edge. Sammy put a finger to his lips to quiet his little brothers. Merle, absorbed in memories, didn't realize they had all slipped in, sitting opposite him, at the other end of the massive room.

Everything Sammy had shared seemed to be true about the old hobo. He had been a soldier, a drover, a lover, and he'd shot a man in Texas. But it was the last verse that touched their hearts deeply.

> Lived my life in a boxcar, since losin' that Kentucky girl.
> But I met Jesus in Utah, and he's takin' care of Merle.
> Little blue-eyed Indian boy—takin' care of Merle.

The family sat stunned as Merle opened his eyes and, suddenly self-conscious, set aside the guitar. Quietly he left the room, heading out the front door.

Sam broke the silence, his face somber. "So eet's not so much Sammy got *lost.*" He shook his head. "More – Merle got *found.*" Then he bowed his head and wept.

———

Dellmira was astonished that Sherriff Buckingham had gotten Lucy to eat every drop of porridge. "She usually spits it out after the first few bites. How'd ya do it?"

Buck snickered. "Oh, it was nothin'. Guess she just likes me." Nobody needed to know he had stirred a spoonful of sugar in it.

Despite the circumstances, Sheriff Buckingham and his posse were settling into a routine. During the day, Dellmira, Louella, and Hallie helped Martha in the kitchen and the boys with chores. In the afternoon, everyone took a nap. At three o'clock, the Jacob girls came down stairs, transformed—mostly—into Buck's posse.

They would saddle their horses and ride to the Montagues' homestead, check the house and livestock, then ride to Reed's place and do the same, looking for anything out of place. The remainder of the evening they patrolled the town, checking the buildings, front and back, and lighting a lamp inside each. After a supper break, came the long night of guarding a short town. They would be stationed in three strategic locations then rotate. Obviously, the bank took priority. "Someone always gotta be watchin' the bank," Buck ordered. "And Hank, you need ta stay on yer horse." Maybe she would appear bigger, he reasoned.

As night after boring night dragged on, the posse got a little lax, falling asleep or meeting in the middle to chat a spell. Del left for thirty minutes around two each morning to feed the baby. Martha was like a grandmother to the child and even Sheriff Buckingham was warming up to the little thing. About the middle of the second week, after Buck had routinely fed her sugar-laced porridge, Lucy leaned from Martha's arms one day, reaching for the sheriff. "Papa!" Buck rolled his eyes and took her out to see the cows.

By the third week, when Sheriff Buckingham walked into the dining room one afternoon, he found the ladies quilting. Martha had brought a quilt top from home and had discovered a quilting frame in the storage closet. They were chatting away, laughing, sipping tea, and having a grand time. "This ain't no tea party, Martha," he said through clenched teeth. "You 'men' go on duty in less than an hour. And ya better be alert!" At the sound of his voice, Lucy crawled out from under the quilt frame. "Papa?"

On patrol that night, the posse could hardly stay awake. Louie had fallen asleep on the porch of the leather shop at one end of town. Del had left her post, to check on the baby. Hank, trying not to fall off her horse, for being so tired, was stationed in the shadows of the church building, watching the bank across the road. She fought sleep, dozing off but waking with each move of the horse. She was in a stupor when Roy lifted his head with alertness. Her eyes scanned the bank. Nothing. Again, Roy's ears perked up. Was that movement over there? On the porch? Hank's heart started pounding, adrenaline bringing her fully awake. Then, she saw him. A tall man, peering in through the window, his silhouette a dark outline in the dim lamplight from inside the bank. She slid off her horse, quiet as a mouse, and felt for her pistol. In this state of emergency, she had forgotten the signal they had practiced, hooting like an owl, to send an alert for backup.

Though shaking with fear, she slipped up behind the dirty outlaw and poked the pistol in the man's back. "Hands in the air!" Hank commanded, in her deepest voice, which wasn't all that deep. The man had startled, but complied lifting his hands. Her mind was racing; she needed to cuff him. "Hands behind your back!" she amended. Hmmm. His hands were inches below the pistol, which was just above his belt.

The man cleared his throat. "Look, I can explain my bein' here." He started to turn toward her.

"Don't move!"

"Listen. I'm a US marshal."

"Yeah, right. And I'm the Queen of England," she proclaimed in her regular voice. Oops.

Hank wasn't sure what to do next. She couldn't manage holding the gun and cuffing him at the same time. In her struggle, she slipped her own hand through one of the cuffs so she could hold the gun while locking the bad guy in the other one. When all was said and done, they were handcuffed—together. He turned toward her then, taking his chances.

As her eyes moved up his tall lanky frame, they landed on a badge. US marshal. Hank lowered the gun. How would she ever explain to Sheriff Buckingham? She was only doing her duty after all, and here she was, handcuffed to a very handsome US marshal.

His deep voice reflected a bit a humor. "Maybe you could find the key and unlock us?" He lifted her right arm with his left.

"Yes, sir," she said in her regular voice, her big brown eyes begging for mercy. "Uh, the key. I keep it in my jewelry box."

# Chapter 32

"Here they come!" Jake announced. Max and Kate's oldest was ten now, and had grown like a weed. He couldn't wait to see his big brothers, Josh and Joey.

The Thatcher Springs bunch scurried around gathering the little ones and trying to form a receiving line like Millie had had them rehearse, just to give order and not miss greeting anyone. Instead, when the Baker City group started up the front steps, utter chaos broke out.

Josh had made it to the porch just as Kate burst through the crowd and pulled him into a tight hug around the middle. "Oh, my Josh," she cried. "I've been worried sick about you!" She wouldn't let him go, and Josh was equally emotional hugging back.

Max gently pried them apart, signaling with his eyes toward Britta, who was smiling happily at the sight. Josh had family who loved him. Kate recovered, wiped her eyes, and blew her nose with a hanky. Before introductions could be made, Joe appeared and started the whole thing all over. "Oh, my Joey," Kate burst into tears again. "I've been worried about you too, sweetheart. This whole shootin' thing had to be so hard on you." Kate had still not acknowledged the beautiful blonde girls, standing to the side.

In unison, Josh and Joe reached for their wives and proudly introduced them to Kate and Max and the kids, who stared at Betsy and Britta like they had never seen twins before. "They're so pretty!" exclaimed little seven-year-old Annie.

Millie appeared in the doorway. "Well, for heaven's sake, are y'all gonna stand out here all day?"

Introductions continued inside, the women remarking at the attractive room. Kate and Uncle Charlie hadn't seen each other for years, and more tears were shed from the memories. He reminded Kate so much of her papa, Clayton. Eula Mae was beside herself with each new member of the family she met. "Oh my! You're all so lovely."

Jack and Lefty approached Millie after the adults had thinned out from being crowded around her. Very properly as always, Jack introduced himself and his friend Lefty. He extended his right hand, Lefty his left. Millie grabbed both their hands at once. Very seriously she said, "Well, boys, we don't shake hands around here." Two sets of eyes grew wide. "We only give hugs!" She pulled them into a big hug, squeezing tightly. "I'm so glad to meet you! Now, how 'bout you two run to the kitchen, right through there," she pointed, "and help Tom serve cookies."

Silas knew his wife was in heaven. He looked around the room at the wonderful mixture of folks: Millie and Sloan who had met for the first time, chatting away easily, laughing. Josh and Britta, Joe and Betsy, a remarkable sight—two sets of newlywed twins. Sam, a dark-eyed Indian, and Grace, her blue eyes sparkling, sat with their three "wild Indians." Charlie and Eula Mae were visiting with Max and Kate, while Jake and Ruthie sat on the floor eating cookies. Annie stood smack dab in front of Betsy and Britta, staring at their every move. Little Max was turning summersaults in the middle of the floor. Pierre and Simone, Margot and her betrothed, Clay Johnson, were next and Andre and Louis, now young men, tall and handsome. Little Toney, with his two-front teeth missing, wandered over to Merle, who sat off by himself, near the tall windows. Ike and Lila Penrose were sitting with Kitty and her husband, Wade. Tom

Carter walked in from the kitchen with two more pitchers of sweet tea and took a seat next to them.

Silas cleared his throat. "Ya'll are probly anxious ta settle in yer rooms, er—suites—but wonder if we could take a little time ta say a few words. Just so us Thatcher Springs folks can know you Baker folks better."

Millie spoke up, "By the way, just so ya know, supper will be served in the dinin' room at six." She looked up at Silas, who signaled her to keep talkin'. "And, well, I just wanta say, I'm so thankful ta God for all of you bein' here. Thank you for makin' the effort." She looked at Josh and Joe and got choked up. "And I thank you Baker folks for takin' good care of our boys." Millie paused to regain composure. "And I thank the Lord for addin' such beautiful young women, Betsy and Britta, to our family. I hope you young folks will share the way it all came about!" She laughed with tears streaming. "We never dreamed when those boys left …" Millie couldn't continue.

Sloan put her arm around Millie's shoulder. "I have ta say, when the Reed boys came ta town, life changed for a lot of us! Changed for the better. We just didn't know it for a while."

"Somethin ya need to know," Josh said quietly. "Before Britta was my wife, she was my doctor." He squeezed her hand. "Britta got me walkin' again." Everyone grew quiet. "She's a purty little thing, but let me tell ya, she's tough as nails."

"Well," Joe spoke up. "She comes by it honestly. My Betsy here was taken hostage by the no-account that shot Josh. Poor sap didn't know who he was dealin' with!" Betsy looked embarrassed and wacked her husband on the arm.

"And Miss Sloan," Josh shook his head. "She was 'Kate' to me, took me in, took care of me when I couldn't take care of myself." Joe was nodding in agreement, smiling at Sloan. "And Eula Mae was like a well-dressed angel!" he exclaimed. "We greeted the Lord together, every morning at sunrise." Josh laughed, then looked over at Jack. "God sends help in all sizes. C'mere, Jack." Jack got up from his seat. Josh pulled him onto his knee. "Jack here is my best buddy. Him and Joey and me, well, we're more like triplets!" he laughed.

Jack, in his grown-up way, said, "Josh is my buddy and my brother all right, but even more, he's like my dad. I never knew my real father. But Josh—well, he's taught me how to be strong and brave. And he taught me how to rope!"

———

Meanwhile, back in Thatcher Springs, Sheriff Buckingham walked out on the porch just before dawn. He was wearing his long handles and carrying a lamp. The dogs had alerted him to some commotion outside.

"Howdy, Sheriff!" US Marshal Ty McAllister walked toward the inn, Hank walking closely beside him.

"Marshal? What are *you* doin' here? What in tarnation is goin' on?" As the marshal and Hank walked up the steps, Buck got a suspicious feeling. He raised the lamp and attempted to walk around behind the two, as it seemed they were hiding something. The more he tried to get behind them, the more they turned to keep the good sheriff in front of them.

Hallie was being convinced to confess. "It's my fault, Sheriff Buckingham. I didn't know he was the marshal," she began. Ty McAllister cut her off.

"This uh, fella, was just doin' her job. *His* job. You can be proud, Sheriff. The thing is, we uh, got cuffed together."

Buck shot Hank a look. "I told ya ta stay on yer horse!" he said through clamped teeth, then pinched the bridge of his nose, hollering for Martha to bring coffee.

Hallie tried to explain, "We were just goin' up to my room. Well, not to my *room* exactly, but the key—the key, to the handcuffs—is in my jewelry box." She gave way to tears. Marshal McAllister lifted the hat off her head. Brunette curls tumbled over her shoulders.

Ty had known she was a girl the whole time. Now he could see she was a downright pretty girl. "I think you're very courageous, Hank."

By the time, Hallie had unlocked the handcuffs that had bound her with the fine-looking marshal, Martha had started breakfast. Suddenly they realized that Lou hadn't returned from duty. Dellmira walked out on the porch, looking down the road through town. An uneasy feeling came over her. Louella's horse was walking toward her, dragging the reins. Louella was nowhere in sight.

While Delmira and Hallie went out to look for Louella, the marshal and the sheriff discussed the situation over breakfast. Buck was embarrassed to admit his posse had turned up three brown-eyed women. And a baby. "It ain't been as bad as I figured. Not so much as a tumbleweed passed through town since we been here, and we only got a week ta go."

"Well, don't let your guard down, Buck. Somethin *is* about to happen in this town. That's what brought me here." Ty went on to explain that while in Laramie to pick up a prisoner, he got wind that the Dalton gang was planning to hit Thatcher Springs Bank. "I have reason to believe they're hid out in the hills somewhere." He motioned toward the end of town.

Suddenly the door burst open. "She's gone! Louella is gone!"

# Chapter 33

The weather at the Oregon coast had been a mixture of rain and sun, dictating the family's activities. That day promised clear skies, a perfect morning to give the children their presents of kites, beach balls, and sand buckets. While families lingered over breakfast, Millie had dozed off in the big wingback chair, by the fireplace in the gathering room. She had a peaceful smile on her lips, the hum of conversation, calming.

In her state of relaxation, gradually Millie felt a presence. She slowly opened her eyes to see a little girl standing before her. The child looked to be a three-year-old angel in a white dress. Red curls sprang out around her cherub face. Millie's heart skipped a beat. Without looking beyond, she softly said, "Well, who have we here?" Millie leaned forward. The room went quiet.

"My name is Millie Mitchel," the child said shyly.

"What do ya know about that!" Millie clapped her hands together. "My name is Millie Mitchel too!" She gently pulled little Millie onto her lap.

The child looked puzzled. "But Papa said your name is Grandma."

Millie looked up then to see the most beautiful site in the world. There in the archway stood Pastor Cody Mitchel, her handsome son and his beautiful wife Lila. Bursting with joy, Millie stood to receive them. Cody took his daughter in one arm and embraced Millie with the other. Lila wrapped her arms around them all. Happy tears flowed. It had been Millie and Silas who God used to turn Cody's life around. And God had used Cody to make that glad reunion possible.

———

The youngsters were having the time of their lives playing on the beach. The older ones flew kites, while keeping eyes on the little ones. Their laughter rang through the French doors like music, as seagulls soared above.

With the children outside, the conversation inside grew to deeper matters. Max noticed that Merle had pulled in a bit closer, listening.

Merle was quite dumbfounded over the yarns he was hearing. Could they even be true? Silas had once been an outlaw? And had taken Miss Kate hostage? The twin girls, Britta and Betsy, separated for seventeen years? And what about Sammy's mama, kidnapped by Indians and now married to one? And that Reed boy, shot in the back by a bank robber! There was no mistake how much they loved each other. Every time they gathered in that big, fancy room, Merle learned more stories and witnessed even deeper love. Of course, those folks were religious people; they believed in God. And still, they were regular folks. When Merle heard Cody's story how he'd met Silas in jail, and now was a preacher, and how Lila discovered her birth mother had been a saloon girl, Merle could hardly take it in. *There's somethin about them people. Can't quite put a finger on it.*

Later, after the noontime meal, Sammy invited Merle down to the beach. "Wanta fly my kite, Uncle Merle?" Merle nodded and followed the boy down the steps, along with several other kite fliers. The salty air felt good; the sun shone brightly. Sammy ran with expertise until the kite lifted and the boy let out more string. The winds at last carried the colorful paper kite high in the sky. Sammy handed the spool over to Merle. "I got it started for ya, Uncle Merle.

Go ahead and fly it all ya want." Merle was smiling; even a chuckle escaped now and then. *Ol' Merle is flyin' a kite.*

After ten minutes of smooth sailing, the kite took a dip and Merle, with Sammy's instructions, wound the string to tighten the slack. Evidently, he hadn't been fast enough as the kite dove and circled wildly and then crashed into a pile of driftwood, shattering to bits, balsa wood and yellow paper scattered about. "Oh no!" Merle exclaimed. "I wrecked yer kite." Merle was visibly upset. "Somehow, I'll get ya new one, Sammy. I'm really sorry."

Sammy solemnly looked at the remains of his kite, then smiled up and Merle. "It's okay, Uncle Merle. I forgive ya."

Something struck Merle. *That's it. That's the common thread in all them stories. Forgiveness.'*

———

Sheriff Buckingham was in a tither over the marshal's report about the Dalton gang. On top of that, they had taken Louella hostage. Martha started crying and Hallie was blaming herself for everything. Marshal McAllister advised everyone to calm down. They needed to come up with a plan.

Dellmira spoke up. "Louella is quiet, but she's the best one ta kidnap, between us three." They all stared at her. "She's smart and she grew up with a passel of brothers. Those outlaws don't stand a chance. Don't need ta worry none about Louella. She'll slip 'em like a cat. Besides, she carries a Derringer in her boot."

———

Clancy Dalton was on duty, making sure their captive didn't escape the hideout, a cave in the hills a couple miles east of Thatcher Springs. When they had realized, their hostage was a woman, they decided that was even better. She would be their cover when they cleaned out Thatcher Springs Bank. They referred to Louella as "Lady Luck." Clancy leaned back against the opening of the cave.

With his body, he blocked the entrance, no chance of her escape. The other two Dalton boys were zonked out in the back of the cave. Louella had been planning her escape since the minute they had grabbed her. With hands tied behind her back, she feigned being frightened. It was time to make her move. Clearing her throat, she said, "Uh, excuse me. I uh, need ta use the privy."

Clancy laughed harshly. "Well, sister, ya got yer choice of them two trees, right over yonder. And make it snappy! Two minutes."

"You'll need ta untie my hands," Louella pleaded. "Just for two minutes."

He looked doubtful, scratching the stubble on his chin, and then an idea hit him. "Tell ya what, sister," he began. "I'm gonna fix ya up with these dandy spurs o' mine." He unbuckled his spur straps, thinking how brilliant he was. His fancy spurs were equipped with jingle bobs. He would be able to hear every move she made.

Once the spurs were strapped to Louella's boots, he untied her hands. "Two minutes!"

Sure enough, every step Louella took jingled as she headed for the biggest Ponderosa. About the time Clancy realized he hadn't heard the jingle bobs in a while, the Dalton gang's horses streaked by the cave, crashing through the brush. Clancy shouted a string of curses as he lumbered out to the tree. There, on the other side, neatly stood Louella's boots, jingle bob spurs and all.

She had shoved the Derringer in her hip pocket, smacked the horses, and took off like a wild cat, leaping from rock to rock and running through the sagebrush in her stocking feet. On the way out of town, Louella had paid attention to various landmarks and knew she was headed back to Thatcher Springs. It was nearly dark, but the pale moon gave her all the light she needed to find her way back.

Finally, she came to the riverbed and followed it upstream, keeping to the brush along the edge. Once she was well out of range, she stopped to catch her breath and gulp water from the river. Louella couldn't help but chuckle at the thought of the Dalton gang running all over tarnation to catch their horses.

# Chapter 34

On the third day of the family reunion, a coach pulled up carrying Gus and Pearl. Kate rushed out the entrance doors to greet her missionary sister. Tom Carter was right on her heals to welcome his younger brother.

Uncle Charlie was about to bust with happiness, never dreaming he'd see his nieces again. He took Eula Mae by the hand, first ones to welcome the couple inside. Gus was clearly holding a sleeping child wrapped in a pink blanket. Millie and Silas looked at each other. *They had a baby?*

Millie stood as the couple entered. "What in the world have ya got there?"

"This is your 'present' from China, Millie." The little one was still in her father's arms. Pearl pealed the blanket back to reveal a sleeping Chinese baby. Her black hair was cut straight across her forehead. Dark almond eyes blinked open, and a chubby hand went to her mouth as she stared out at the room full of people. "Please meet our daughter, Jia Li." Pearl's eyes glistened. "Her name means, 'Good and beautiful.'"

Britta had sucked in a breath at the sight of the little Chinese girl. Josh put his arm around her, pulling her to his side, as they sat on a sofa across the room. Only he had known about Liu, the heartbreak his wife had suffered. He kissed her hair. "You okay, sweetheart?" She nodded, but he felt the tension in her shoulders, as she tried to hold back tears.

That afternoon Will and Ada, along with Freddie and Liz, arrived, the last of the family. Everyone had come! The two couples had met in Portland and spent the night there to rest up from their long journey. Ada was quite pregnant and looked radiant. All three of Kate's sisters had thoroughly changed from that long-ago day when they had arrived in Thatcher Springs, overdressed and overdramatic. Joe leaned over to whisper something to Josh. "Remember when we put Cayenne pepper in their gravy?"

Betsy overheard. "You didn't!"

Josh laughed. "That ain't all. Before that, we scared 'em near to death with a spider this big!" He made a circle with his hand.

The twin wives looked at each other in astonishment. Then all four muffled a laugh.

Ada spotted them across the room. "There you are! You bad, naughty boys." The sisters were laughing heartily, but Ada continued, "We've come for revenge. You two better watch your backs! And your gravy."

The afternoon was spent sharing more stories and passing around the little china doll. At last Britta got to hold her, cooing and crying and laughing all at once. "Oh Josh. Isn't she beautiful?" Britta held the child and rocked her, not wanting to let go.

After supper that night, when the families made their way to the gathering room, they were surprised to see the rugs rolled back, set aside. The furniture had been pushed back as well. "Everyone go ahead and take a seat," Millie requested. "Silas and I have gift to give." Silas reached behind his chair and pulled out a long rectangular box wrapped in silver paper and tied with a white chiffon ribbon. Millie held the box like something fragile was inside. "This is a very late wedding gift of sorts." She paused. "Lila dear? It's for you." She lifted the box toward Lila.

Cody smiled proudly at his wife, who seemed to be frozen in place. "Go ahead, honey. She said it's for you."

Ike and Esther Penrose smiled humbly, so delighted in their daughter.

Lila sat on the arm of Millie's chair and slowly peeled the wrapping paper back. When she opened the box, she gasped in unreserved amazement. She looked up at her husband, still smiling even though he didn't know the meaning of the gift. Millie explained.

"Henry Weaver was the first person to show up on my doorstep in Thatcher Springs, many years ago. He's gone on to glory now, but Henry was my lifesaver, a black man, a slave from the south. Henry made the sweetest music from this old violin. It had been given him by his master, after Henry had saved the man's son from a herd of stampedin' cattle."

"When Cody told me—a long time back—how Lila had lost her violin to a horse wreck, I determined to have Henry's restored for her. It's taken all this time, just findin' someone to bring it back to life. Turns out it's a fine instrument, built in Italy. Don't think Henry ever knew that."

Silas spoke up. "Lila, honey? Would ya play us somethin'"?

Lila couldn't quit hugging Millie and Silas, filled with gratitude. Finally, she stood holding the violin like it was made of glass and began to tune it, listening with a keen ear until it was perfect. She walked across the floor to stand by Cody.

Ike whispered to his wife, "Bet she plays a hymn."

"Or maybe Mozart." Esther was lost in memories.

The room had gone completely silent, all eyes on Lila. Slowly, she raised Henry's polished violin, to her chin. She lifted the bow and shot a smile at Cody. Her foot started tapping. "A *one* and a *two* and a ..." With her head bobbing and red curls springing, to everyone's delight, she broke into "Cotton-Eyed Joe!" After all, this was Henry's violin.

The Thatcher Springs kids knew exactly what to do; they ran out on the dance floor and started dancing. Then, Uncle Charlie stood and offered his arm to Eula Mae. "Care to cut a rusty, darlin?"

"Oh Charles! How lovely."

It didn't take long for others to follow suit. Max and Kate got right in the swing of things, followed by Joe and Britta. Before long Sam and Grace, then Millie and Silas until the place was vibrating. Lefty dared Jack to cut in on Uncle Charlie. They were both tugging on her, but Charlie gave Eula Mae up to her grandson.

Wade McKenzie led his reluctant wife to the piano and soon, her red curls were springing too. Merle, in his usual corner, strummed the guitar, tapping his toe, smiling.

After several rounds, the dancers were relieved to take a break. Tom wheeled in a cart from the kitchen, laden with pitchers of cold lemonade, made with California lemons, and sugar cookies. Sloan had offered to help with cooking that day, while the chef made a run for supplies. She and Tom served the refreshments.

Max leaned in and whispered something to Kate, motioning toward Josh and Joe. "They might be married men, but they're still schemers. I can read 'em like a book. Wonder what their plannin' over there." Jack seemed to be in on it. After a bit, Max and Kate observed Jack casually walk over to speak with Lila. She nodded.

A glass of lemonade later, Jack worked his way over to Kitty at the piano, said a few words, and sauntered on over to Britta, who was sitting with Pearl, holding little Jia Li. She smiled at Jack and handed the baby over to its mother. The music started up again, only this time, a slow number, a waltz. All attention went to Josh, who was slowly getting up from his chair, leaning on his cane. He stood for a moment, got his bearings, and then set the cane aside. Jack stepped up next him, making sure his friend was steady. Slowly, Josh walked to the middle of the floor, where Britta stood waiting. Josh placed his hands on her shoulders; she put her hands at his waist. They looked in each other's eyes, swaying to the music as if no one was in the room. Tears sprung as Britta smiled, looking up at her husband. *Thank you, Lord, for this miracle.*

# Chapter 35

Marshal McAllister joined "Del" and "Hank" for night duty. He would watch the bank, and the other two would stay together near the end of town. "I hope Louella's all right." Hallie was more worried than the others seemed to be.

"She'll be fine, Hallie. Don't worry." Dellmira changed the subject. "I notice ya been eyein' the young marshal."

"I have not! He's a very nice gentleman. That's all." Hallie had her dander up.

"Fine lookin' too," Dellmira taunted.

"Dellmira. Quit it!" Hallie was glad it was dark; her cheeks were hot, turning pink.

From a distance came, "Hoot hoot."

"What in heaven's name?" Hallie peered into the darkness beyond town.

Dellmira didn't skip a beat. She cupped her hands. "Hoot hoot."

A shadow appeared from the brush. Louella!

The three girls hugged a giggled, sounding nothing like the posse of men they were supposed to be. "Are ya all right, Lou?" Dellmira had been more worried than she had let on. "Did they rough ya up? How'd ya get away?"

Later at breakfast, Louella filled everyone in on what she knew about the Dalton gang. She had listened when they thought she was asleep, observed what guns and ammunition they carried and condition of their horses. "If they ever *find* their horses!" She laughed. "Truth is, the Daltons are three not so bright outlaws." She shook her head and went on to tell them how she escaped.

"So, you think they's still gonna hit the bank?" Buck asked.

"Yep. And I figure it'll be tonight. They think the Thatcher Springs folks are on their way back. Kept sayin' they had ta act fast. They've been eyeing the town from a distance. Know all of us is here. All except the marshal. They don't know he came ta town."

Marshal McAllister took the lead in their plan making, laying out a strategy. When they had it figured out, he said, "It's gonna be a long night. Ya'll better get some rest. Let's meet back here at four, prepared, with guns and ammunition." He looked at each one. "You ladies can shoot, right?"

"That's the one thing I can say fer 'em marshal. They can definitely shoot. All three of 'em. That was the first thing we did, the day they showed up." Buck displayed a bit of pride. "Yep. I made sure of that."

Everyone went off in different directions. Louella, to heat water for a bath. Dellmira took the baby upstairs. Hallie helped Martha clear the table and wash dishes in the kitchen. Buck went out back to break the news to his sons. They would be ecstatic. The two boys would take part in the ambush.

Hallie returned to the dining room, and not expecting anyone, was startled when Ty cleared his throat. He was standing by the hearth. "You headin' up to rest a bit?"

"Not really. I'm too keyed up about tonight." Hallie couldn't look directly at him. She fiddled with the button on her shirtsleeve. It was just the two of them in the dining room.

"Care ta join me for a little ride? I wanta check the sight, mark our posts for tonight." Ty was staring at her.

"Uh sure. That would be nice. I'll get my coat and hat." She hesitated, "Should I pull my hair up under my hat? Or am I gonna be a girl on this ride?" Shyly she smiled up at him.

"You're gonna be a girl either way. A very pretty one, I might add." He smiled a smile that melted her.

They rode in silence for a spell, climbing a trail behind the Reed cabin, where Sam Weaver and his family now lived. From high in the hills, they could see the layout of Thatcher Springs, the small town, the Montagues' place to the west, and Max and Kate's homestead in the distance, straight ahead. Ty pointed eastward, the place where the Daltons were holed up, according to Louella. "She musta trekked along the river for a at least two, maybe three miles down there."

"Louella is strong. So is Dellmira. They're married to my two older brothers. I just came along for the ride. Seemed like an adventure." She paused, looking straight ahead. "I'm not really cut out for this job."

"But you can shoot, right?"

She nodded, smiling up at him as they sat side by side in their saddles. "Oh yeah. I can shoot."

"And we know you can handcuff a man—when the need arises." He was grinning boyishly.

She felt her face flush. "Marshal McAllister, sir," she began. He didn't let her finish.

"Just call me Ty. And how 'bout I call you Hallie?" Their eyes locked. "I didn't mind bein' handcuffed—not one bit. Specially to a beautiful woman."

By the time they were back at the inn, Ty had marked two places along the upper trail where the Buckingham boys would be posted. They would handle real guns—but not real bullets. Ty would outfit them with blanks.

Martha would be stationed downhill some ways, not too far from the inn, with a shotgun. "You bet she knows what ta do with it." Sheriff Buckingham had bragged. "A feller better mind his p's and q's around my Martha."

Dellmira would remain inside the inn, keeping her baby safe, but a window at the end of the building closest to town would be cracked open, giving space for another shotgun, still providing cover.

Louella and Hallie would be located opposite each other, in-between buildings, Louella in the shadows next to the bank and Hallie by the church.

Tensions were high just before dusk, when they took their positions. All except for Hallie. She couldn't quit thinking about Ty McAllister, their ride earlier that day. She was musing at his handsome good looks, deep blue eyes, his strong jaw, broad shoulders. He was tall and—

"Hallie!" Her thoughts were broken. The handsome marshal was hollering at her. "Are ya ready?" He walked toward her at her post by the church. "Don't leave this spot—even if shootin' begins. I don't want anything ta happen to ya, girl." With tenderness, he touched her cheek, then hurried back to his post inside the bank.

They didn't have to wait long. Before dark, the Dalton gang raced into town, guns blazing. They had decided on the *element of surprise* tactic, but just before they reached the bank, guns started firing from every direction. Their horses came to a halt in the middle of the road, spinning and bucking in fear. "What in tarnation?" Clancy couldn't believe their luck.

Hallie gasped as she watched Marshal McAllister step off the porch of the bank, and stand directly in front of the three outlaws, still horseback. He had both guns drawn. "Hold it right there, boys."

Clancy shouted out some curse words, eyeing the badge on Ty's vest. They had counted on three men and "lady luck" being their only obstacle. Instead, they were surround by an army of guns and a US marshal.

Clancy would not be outsmarted. Quickly he pulled a match from between his teeth and struck it on his pant leg with one hand, holding a bundle of dynamite in the air with the other. It appeared to have a short fuse. He lit it, laughing harshly, exposing tobacco-stained teeth.

Hallie leaned against the church building, saying a prayer. She was in direct line to Clancy, holding the dynamite above his head. The other two Daltons looked skittish over what Clancy was about to do. *Help me, Lord. Help me be accurate.* With two hands, little Hallie Jacobs aimed her pistol. She felt confident, steady. Bam!

The dynamite flew to the ground, fuse still burning with inches to go. The gang spun on their horses racing out of town. Clancy held his wounded arm to his belly.

In split seconds, Ty grabbed the bundle that was about to explode and ran like a racehorse right past Louella, next to the bank. He heaved the bundle of dynamite with everything he had far out behind the buildings.

Hallie screamed, "Ty! No!" and ran across the road right past Louella, still in shock. She collided with Ty on his retreat from the soon to be explosion. He pulled her to the ground, sheltering her with his body, just in time. The explosion rocked the town of Thatcher Springs. Everyone crouched, frozen in place.

With her face smashed in the dirt, Hallie opened one eye. She was inches away from Ty's face, their noses almost touching. He was pretty much on top of her. They had come close to death. She licked the dust from her lips. "You saved us," she whispered.

Ty helped her stand, but didn't let her go. He pulled her into his strong arms. "No, sweetheart, *you* saved *us*."

# Chapter 36

Sometime after the waltz, Sloan and Tom brought more refreshments from the kitchen, including a spread of Sloan's pies. With her back to the room, she arranged them on a buffet table against the wall. Josh noticed something and whispered to Britta, who whispered to Betsy who gasped and whispered to Joe. They laughed as if sharing a private joke. Unknown to Sloan, a white handprint, like flour, appeared on her blue dress, at the small of her back. "Looks ta me like a little waltzin' goin' on in the kitchen!" exclaimed Josh. "Better keep an eye on those two."

Tom Carter was in his early fifties. His salt and pepper hair was thick and wavy and his eyes warm brown. He loved to hunt and fish and knew how to prepare his bounty, creating wonderful aromas from the kitchen. He was polite, though quiet, and he and Sloan worked well together. He had been impressed by the way she turned out beautiful loaves of bread and thought nothing of whipping up ten pies. It was not lost on him she was also a beautiful woman. Sloan had been dumbstruck, when he had asked her to dance. "In the kitchen?" she had asked laughing, but as the music floated in, he led her in a waltz around the chopping block in the middle of the room.

Sam had walked out to the porch, to check the youngsters on the beach below. He leaned on the rail with interest. His three boys along with Max and Kate's bunch, Jack and Lefty and little Tony Montague, were sitting in the sand, gathered around Merle, who sat on a driftwood log. They were circled around a small campfire. Merle seemed to be telling a story. He motioned for Sammy and Jake to stand next to each other then walk out until they were about five feet apart. Even from a distance, Sam could tell that the kids were astonished at whatever Merle had said. The old hobo got a big kick out of it, chuckling.

Later Sammy and Jake excitedly told their families all about Texas Longhorns. They paced off as they had done on the beach, to demonstrate the length from tip to tip, of one horn to the other. "Uncle Merle is really smart!" exclaimed Jake. All the youngsters were now calling him "Uncle Merle." Merle remained quiet when with the adults, just listening, taking it in. To the children, he was comfortable, a hero of sorts with all his curious yarns.

Although it was only midmorning, Millie rang the dinner bell. "Just have a few announcements!" she exclaimed. "This evenin' after supper, we're plannin' a sing-along. Y'all be thinkin' of your favorites. And then on Friday—anybody wonder why these frames are empty?" She motioned to the walls. Hands shot up, mostly from the younger generation. Millie laughed. "Friday, a real professional photographer is comin! He will shoot portraits of individual families as well as one big picture of this whole bunch of beautiful people." She pointed to the huge frame above the mantel. "So right after lunch, please show up in this room dressed for the picture takin'. And Britta and Betsy, put on yer weddin' dresses, darlin's. And twinners, be wearin' yer suits! Yer weddin' reception will be that evening. That's on Friday."

Just then, the inn's chef approached Millie with another announcement to share. Millie looked excited. "Chef Springer says tomorrow mornin'—real early—the tide will be extra low, for anybody who wants ta go clam diggin'! He's willin' ta take ya out and provide buckets and shovels." She turned and asked something of the chef. "And he'll show ya how!"

Jack and Lefty couldn't wait for morning and ran out to the beach to scout for razor clams. Eventually a breeze kicked up and soon all the youngsters were out flying their kites, the little ones playing in the sand. Sammy ran over to Merle. "Ya wanta go clam diggin' in the morning, Uncle Merle?"

Merle ruffed up the boy's hair. "Reckon so, Sammy. Least ta watch."

The boy grinned up at his old buddy. "Let's go fly the kite!"

"Don't tell me ya patched her up?" Merle asked with disbelief.

"Naw. That one's a gonner. Jack Witherspoon gave me his."

———

Buck walked in the back door holding Lucy. "Listen ta this, Martha." Lucy grabbed his nose. "Lucy," the sheriff said sweetly, "what's a cow say?" The baby kept grabbing at his nose. "C'mon, sweetheart, what's a cow say?" Martha had never heard her husband talk so sweetly. "Tell Papa. What's a cow say?"

It finally sunk in. The baby looked at Martha and said in perfect English, "Mooooo."

Buck threw his head back and laughed. "Ain't she somethin'?" A cat slinked by. "Lucy! What's a kitty say?" Buck demonstrated. "Meee-ooooww." Martha laughed heartily—more at Buck.

The girls walked in, nudging each other at the sight. Dellmira took the baby. "Thanks for watchin her, Papa. And thanks to both of you for putting up with all of us. It must've been a big letdown, when we first rode in. Us bein' women and all. Louella and Hallie and me wanta prepare supper tonight, give Martha a break and to celebrate runnin' off the Dalton gang."

Ty had been helping the boys with chores. For some reason, he hadn't seemed in a big hurry to leave Thatcher Springs. "Somebody say somethin' about a party?" he asked as he entered the kitchen, winking at Hallie.

Everyone delighted in the meal of fried chicken, sweet glazed carrots, and chocolate cake. It was *supposed* to be cake, but when Hallie pulled it from the oven it sunk into more of a gooey mess. Dished up in bowls and topped with fresh cream, however, it was a smashing success. "This is the best chocolate puddin' I ever ate!" Ty directed his compliment at Hallie.

After supper, Martha and Buck and their two boys relaxed by the fire, entertained by Lucy who crawled after the cat. "Meee-ooooww," she squealed. Buck was so proud.

The girls were cleaning the kitchen, with Ty's help. When he carried a stack of dishes to the pantry, Ty came out with a banjo. "Where'd this come from?" Tom Carter had left it behind, taking his guitar to the reunion instead. "Anybody play this thing?"

Before long, Hallie was strumming the banjo and the three girls broke into old cowboy songs, their voices in perfect harmony. With a bit of encouragement, the others joined in. There was something about this Thatcher Springs place that brought folks together, feeling like family.

By coincidence, or maybe not, everyone had turned in, leaving Ty and Hallie alone by the fire. Ty added wood, suggesting he planned to stay for a while. Hallie poured fresh coffee. Though awkward at first, the conversation turned easy. Hallie shared life at home with her parents and younger brother on their small ranch. Her two older brothers and their wives, Dellmira and Louella, lived close by.

Ty thoughtfully said, "I been thinkin' for a while ta do somethin different. Settle down. Maybe claim a parcel of land, build a house, run some cows. Marshalin' is a good job, worthy. But lonesome at times too." He looked over at Hallie in the rocking chair next to his.

"You're a brave man, Ty. Dealin' with outlaws all the time. I can understand yer feelin's." Hallie dared a glance at him.

"Thatcher Springs here would be a good spot to settle in. It's quiet and beautiful. Rich soil, good meadowland, the river and all." Ty mused, looking into the fire.

"And now with a lake!" They looked at each other and burst out laughing. The dynamite had created a crater in the ground out behind the town, where springs filled it with freshwater.

Ty reached for her hand. She complied, taking his. He leaned in closer. Their eyes held. He swallowed. He leaned even closer. Hallie leaned toward him. He looked at her lips with longing. Just then, "C'mon sugar, let's find that kitty cat!" Buck was coming downstairs with his sweet Lucy.

When he saw Ty and Hallie, it didn't seem to register that they were about to kiss. "Ya'll seen the cat? Poor little Lucy can't seem ta settle down."

Ty rubbed his chin. "Think he went out with your boys, Sherriff, out to the bunkhouse."

"Well, I'll jest sit with ya'll a spell and rock her to sleep." He sat in the rocker on the other side of Hallie, patting the little one's back, humming.

When suddenly he began to sing "Blood on the Saddle," Hallie looked at Ty with eyes wide. They struggled to keep from laughing out loud. Ironically, Lucy settled down with each verse. Ty whispered, "Let's go in the kitchen."

They tiptoed across the room, slowly pushing open the kitchen door so it wouldn't creak, feeling like kids again. Ty took her hand, leading her into the pantry. Hallie's heart began to race at the realization she was standing in the dark pantry with Ty McAllister. She felt the back of his hand touch her hair. She was thinking she should move away, but couldn't. He shifted in closer until she felt his warm breath against her cheek. "You are beautiful, Hallie," he whispered, and kissed her hair. She tipped her face up just as he leaned in to kiss her lips. She let her arms wrap around him, kissing him back with feeling. They kissed again, passion stirring both hearts.

When they came out of the pantry, Hallie smoothed her hair, smiling. *If Pa knew what just happened in the pantry, he would be shootin' a US marshal.*

# Chapter 37

Jack and Lefty won the clam-digging contest with a bucket full, twenty-six razor clams in all. Once they had figured it out, the two pals had developed a system. They would walk along the wet sand, bent over searching for bubbles, in the dim early light. "Over there!" Jack would dig fast as he could, counting to four, then Lefty would quickly reach, sometimes barely grabbing the clam's neck, pulling it out and throwing it in the bucket. They were a good team. It was because of that, Jack had given his kite to little Sammy. Lefty needed an extra hand for kite flying; they could share one kite.

Sloan and Tom, after the chef had instructed them, spent the morning shucking clams, preparing them to be fried, like chicken, for supper that night. They laughed at the fact they would never again need this skill when they each went back home. "What's it like, Sloan? Your ranch?"

She found herself comfortably telling Tom all about it—from the beginning. She told him about her husband's murder, the birth of her twins, the hardships and struggles. "Thanks to God and Uncle Charlie, then Joe and Josh Reed." She hesitated with emotion. "McLemore Ranch is up again, cows on green grass."

"Ouch!" Tom exclaimed. "No wonder they call 'em razor clams." He had sliced the palm of his hand.

"Let me look at that." Quickly Sloan flushed the wound with clean water and wrapped his hand in a fresh towel. "Stay put, Tom. Be right back." She returned in a few minutes with her medicine kit, and continued doctoring his wound. Their heads were inches apart. When she had applied iodine, she looked up to see his reaction, knowing it would sting. He didn't flinch, but was looking straight at her. Heat flushed her cheeks. She couldn't move.

"You're a very pretty woman, Sloan McLemore." Then in the next breath, "May I kiss you?"

Sloan felt like a young girl, as if it was her very first kiss. What was happening to her? She'd been so caught up in everyone else falling in love, it never occurred to her that she might have a chance at love too, a second chance. Her heart was racing. *Lord, please show me how to handle these feelings. Is this the right thing? Show me, Lord.*

At supper that night, everyone marveled at the delicate, tender goodness of their first fried clams. After they had been served, Sloan and Tom took their plates out on the veranda and shared their meal in the glow of an orange-red and purple sunset sky.

———

They had started out with folk songs, Lila playing the violin and Kitty the piano. Tom insisted Merle go ahead and play his guitar. He knew it gave the old hobo a sense of security, having something to do. Besides, Tom had his attention on Sloan. They discovered their voices blended perfectly.

Eventually the Thatcher Springs bunch began singing "Amazing Grace," the others joining in, catching on to the way the women sang one part, and then the men, then everyone together.

Grace began speaking. Even though others had shared their lives over the past week, she had remained quiet, enjoying everyone else's story. Merle leaned forward. He had been curious about the strikingly beautiful blue-eyed girl, Sammy's mother.

The room went still as she calmly spoke. "My early life, I lived as an Indian, learning to gather and weave—all the things young Indian women do. Sage Blossom," she motioned toward Simone, "cared for me like a mother. But all that time, I knew I didn't belong. For so many years, I didn't know where I belonged. I would lay on my mat at night and sense a *power*. Something greater than myself."

She went on to share how Simone had risked her life to save her from death. How they were on the run for months until Pierre found them. She looked at Pierre with a heart of love, recalling how he had taken them in.

Then, Grace told the amazing story of being reunited with Millie, her true mother. She reached her hand to Millie, sitting next to her. "If not for your endless praying ..." She couldn't finish. Through tears she said, "I love you, Mother."

When Grace finished her testimony, Samuel's eyes pooled with tears. In fact, there wasn't a dry eye in the room. "It's been on my heart these past days, to share my story," she continued. "That 'power'—the Mighty One—was always with me. I struggled to let go, to truly trust him. But when finally I did, blessing after blessing began to pour out on me. I am so grateful for my family, my beautiful boys, and my wonderful husband. And for *both* my mothers." She looked around the room, her eyes spilling over, when they landed on Kate. "Thank you from my heart. I love you all."

Others were prompted to speak freely. Millie told of her first husband, Grace's father, being killed by an Indian arrow, baby Grace abducted. She shared not only her heartbreak but the bitterness that plagued her for many years.

With raw emotion, one after another shared their story. Sloan's heart broke all over again when she told of her babies being separated. Tom gently took her hand.

Joe described the day his brother was shot in the bank robbery, how he struggled with guilt and fear that Josh would never walk again. "It should have been me." His voice was shaky.

Then Cody told them about "a little boy" surviving in the streets of San Francisco, of meeting Silas in jail, of a new life in Thatcher Springs. The strange story of his father leaving him a wealth of gold, the way he met Lila.

Kitty had begun to speak, but emotion overwhelmed her. Wade pulled her close as she cried into his chest. In-between sobs, she whispered something to him. Wade looked out to the crowd, still holding her close. His handsome face broke into a smile. "She wants to tell ya all, that she's 'just so happy!'"

All the while, Merle was taking it in, listening to every word, perceiving every bared soul.

At Pastor Ike's suggestion, they closed the evening with the hymn "Come Thou Fount of Every Blessing." As Merle lay awake on his bed that night, one verse played over and over in his mind.

> O to grace how great a debtor
> Daily I'm constrained to be!
> Let Thy goodness, like a fetter,
> Bind my wandering heart to Thee.
> Prone to wander, Lord I feel it,
> Prone to leave the God I love,
> Here's my heart, O take and seal it,
> Seal it for Thy courts above.

"Here's my heart, Lord," he whispered in the darkness. "Here's ol' Merle's heart."

# Chapter 38

When Kate walked into the gathering room—turned photography studio—she was stunned by Josh and Joe, so handsome in their dark suits, standing with their lovely brides. Britta and Betsy had donned their wedding dresses and arranged each other's hair, as it had been for their wedding day.

Millie stepped up next to her, putting her arm around Kate's waist. The reality was sinking in: their twinners were really married! The photographer, with help from his assistant, got the two couples situated, with the lighting exactly right. It was early enough to capture them standing just inside open French doors, a backdrop of the beautiful Pacific Ocean. After a few takes, Betsy called out to Sloan. "C'mon, Mama, you belong here with us."

Next up, tall and handsome Cody Mitchel, his beautiful Lila and little Millie. They would make a fine portrait. With a bit of flair, the photographer added Ike and Esther to the family, and then Millie and Silas, the parents. Silas was so proud of his son, remembering their first encounter in the county jail. Getting them all to smile came easy.

Sam asked to be next because he wasn't certain how long his boy's white shirts would remain white. Besides. they were jumpy to get out on the beach. As they were being arranged for the shoot,

Sammy ran over and grabbed Merle's hand. "C'mon, Uncle Merle. You're with us."

Sam and Grace both nodded in agreement. "C'mon, Uncle Merle," Sam repeated, with his bright smile. Merle reluctantly joined them, self-conscious, straightening his vest. He couldn't remember ever having his picture taken; there was no one who would want it. Grace was placed in the middle, Sam and Merle on each side, the three boys in front. The photographer seemed extra pleased with this one. "Perfecto!" he nodded to his assistant when the shoot was over.

The Montague family would create another handsome picture, their dark hair gleaming in a shaft of light. They had chosen to wear Indian garments: soft buckskin dresses on the women and tunics of the same buckskin, worn by Pierre and his sons and Margot's fiancé, Clay. Intricate beading embellished their clothing, the handiwork of Simone and Margot.

Nothing but the pink chiffon would do for Eula Mae. Of course, she wore a matching hat, lace gloves, and a fan of pink feathers. "You are the rose among thistles!" remarked the photographer as he arranged Uncle Charlie, Jack, and Lefty around her. "Oh my! How lovely." She whipped open her fan for privacy, as Uncle Charlie stole a kiss.

When it was the Reed family's turn, Kate straightened Ruthie's sash and fluffed Annie's curls, checked the boy's shirts, and slicked down their hair—again. She licked her thumb and wiped a smudge off little Max's cheek. The photographer got them all arranged, but before he went behind his camera, Kate halted everything. "This isn't right. I mean, sir, this is not our whole family." Max read his wife like a book.

"All right. Joshua? Joseph? Bring your wives and get on over here!"

When all other families and couples completed their turns, Silas and Millie walked to the setting for their portrait. Everyone began to clap, shouting, "Thank you!" and "We love you!" The photographer snapped, just as Millie smiled her affection out to everyone, her eyes glistening, Silas smiling down at her with a heart full of love. "Bravo!" exclaimed the photographer. "This one will take a prize!"

At last they gathered everyone and got them arranged for the grand finale, the family portrait to be featured above the mantel. A brass plate, already placed at the bottom of the frame, was engraved, "Glad Reunion—1877."

Cody and Lila would leave in the morning. Cody was scheduled to preach the following week, at a growing church in Sacramento, hoping to become the new pastor. They'd been praying for an appointment closer to both her family in San Francisco, and his, in Thatcher Springs.

The Baker City folks would leave in the afternoon. Josh and Joe convinced Max to arrange their journey, to include a stop in Baker. They had offered Merle a job at McLemore Ranch, but he had already accepted one in Thatcher Springs.

Gus and Pearl would leave the next day too. They were scheduled to visit several churches on their way to board the steamship that would take them back to China. "We will be speaking with these congregations about adopting Chinese babies. There's a continuous flow—mostly baby girls—coming to our orphanage." At this revelation, Josh noticed Britta sit forward a bit, eyes big. Perhaps a seed had been planted.

———

Sloan and Tom outdid themselves setting up a buffet table in the gathering room, for the wedding reception and their last evening together. The table, against the wall as usual, was especially elaborate this time, decorated with silver candelabras on a beautiful floor-length linen cloth. The edge was adorned with a four-inch border, crocheted in matching cream. The children had brought shells from the beach, which were scattered the length of the table, between silver platters of cheese and fruit, pastries and pies and little cakes like they had enjoyed at San Francisco's Grand Hotel. The centerpiece was a three-tiered wedding cake, embellished with pale yellow roses. Pitchers of sweet tea, lemonade, and hot coffee in fancy urns with little spigots completed the sumptuous display.

Silas took the floor. "First off, congratulations to our boys, Josh and Joe, for marryin' the purtiest set of twins I ever seen!" Everyone clapped as the couples kissed. "We wanta pray over 'em and celebrate the biggest event of their lives." He looked over at Millie. "Even though we missed the weddin'!"

The two couples were directed to the middle of the room as the three pastors—Cody, Ike, and Wade—took a turn praying for them.

Silas went on. "I wanta thank y'all—ever single one—fer comin' ta this here shindig. Each of you means the world ta me and Millie. Y'all have made her so happy, comin'. We praise God fer blessin' us so." He reached for Millie's hand and together they started singing. The roomful followed suit, standing, holding hands, their voices filling the room.

> Bless be the tie that binds,
> Our hearts in Christian love.

Some were looking heavenward; others closed their eyes. Silas looked around the circle. Sam's kids seemed to be missing.

> The fellowship of kindred minds,
> Is like to that above.
> They sang it again.

Silas was getting nervous. The "wild Indians" had not caused too much mischief all week, but he couldn't help but wonder. Suddenly he spotted movement under the table, the cloth slightly billowing. *Oh no!* Silas released the hands he held and with a giant leap threw his body toward the end of the table, just as little Henry squirted out from underneath, the crocheted edge catching a button on the back of his britches. As if in slow motion, and to everyone's alarm, the whole cloth went with him, sweet tea tipping off the end of the table. Silas connected with the little guy just as a huckleberry pie went over, splattering them both. A candle toppled, starting a fire on the tablecloth, but by the grace of God, a pitcher of lemonade put it out. The whole thing came to a halt, just as the wedding cake came within inches of the table's edge.

When the dust settled, the other two, Dallas and Sammy, came out from under the table wondering what had happened. The room had gone quiet; the spell of voices harmonizing, had been broken. From the corner of the room came a chuckle. It turned into a full-out hearty laugh. He couldn't seem to stop. It was Uncle Merle. Tears of laughter streaked his face. Every time he tried to collect himself, he burst out laughing again. Before long everyone joined him, the room erupting in laughter.

Just before they headed to bed, Sam and Grace walked with their three boys over to where Millie was seated. "Go ahead. Say it." Sam gave Henry a little nudge forward, evidently the spokesman for the group.

"We sawee Gwama Dahlin, fo weckin' you Gwad Weunion." Millie tried to look serious, but then pulled all three boys into a big hug.

She kissed each one. "Well, bless Pat! I always thought you boys were sweet. Now y'all are *extra* sweet." She licked her lips. "Hmmm. just like huckleberry pie!"

---

Lived my life in a box car, runnin' from that bloody war,
But I found peace with a family, over on the Oregon shore.
I found Jesus with my family, over on the Oregon shore.
Little blue-eyed Indian boy …
Over on that Oregon shore.

# *Epilogue*

## Christmas 1880

Tom Carter and Sloan McLemore had married in November 1877. The Home Cookin' Café had gone up for sale and they bought the place and spent several months revamping the kitchen and redecorating the dining room. The name was slightly changed to Carter's Home Cookin' and featured Sloan's breads and pies. Walls had been paneled with weathered barn boards from McLemore Ranch and all manner of ranching paraphernalia was displayed, including old-time photos of early settlers. Blue-and-white-checkered tablecloths and polished wood floors gave the place a true homey feel.

Most of the time, Tom and Sloan lived in the small apartment above the café, which was included in the sale and remodeled into a cozy suite. The café closed on Sundays and Mondays, giving the joyful couple "family time" at the ranch, with Betsy and Joe, Britta and Josh, and of course their cherished grandchildren.

Betsy had given birth to a beautiful little boy, born in August 1878, and Britta had delivered adorable baby Eddie a month later, on the anniversary of that fateful day at the bank, when Josh was shot in the back. He was thankful and amazed every day, at the way God had brought that bleak event to a jubilant end. He had fully recovered; only a slight limp remained. Britta and Josh felt blessed beyond their wildest dreams as they awaited the arrival of their daughter—coming soon, from China.

The brothers had expanded the main ranch house, adding a wing on each side, one to accommodate Josh and Britta's growing family, and the other private quarters for Sloan and Tom, with a separate room for guests. The place looked more like a sprawling mountain lodge from the road leading to it.

Joe and Betsy loved their little cabin out behind the horse pasture. Someday maybe they would expand, once the sleeping loft was filled with children. For now, the cozy place suited the family fine. Most days Betsy worked alongside Joe, outdoors, little Jonathon right along with them.

With a new roof and repairs to the siding, the barn stood proudly and featured a bunkhouse, with a wood stove and two sets of bunk beds. Jack and Lefty spent much of the summer there and turned out to be mighty fine hands, especially during brandings, when they worked the cows. Jack no longer roped the dummy steer. He was now an expert at the real thing.

———

The church at Thatcher Springs, God's House, had been filled to the brim for the wedding of Hallie Jacobs and Ty McAllister. After that July "posse" job, the three girls had returned to Homestead and just as promised, Ty had shown up two weeks later to speak with Mr. Jacobs about courting his daughter. The wedding took place the following April and the happy couple moved into the Reed cabin. A year later, Hallie gave birth to a brown-eyed daughter, Sophie.

Sam and Grace had claimed land to the east and built a log home like the Montagues, like the one Grace had lived in after she and Simone were rescued by Pierre. They welcomed another boy into the family, who was the delight of his big brothers. They were as excited, as if little Silas Merle had been a new puppy.

Merle had turned out an accomplished hand, knowledgeable about many things on the place. He was good with animals, an able blacksmith, and with his fixing, the cook stove no longer smoked. He lived in Henry's former quarters in the bunkhouse and for the first time in his life felt like he was *home*. He had secretly been working on a project in the shop, a present for the Thatcher Springs young folks. The women had been cooking and baking for days, and Max had chopped down the perfect tree to decorate. It would be Merle's first Christmas. Ever. He was a blessed man.

Kate and Millie were over the moon when the letter came saying Josh and Joe would bring their families "home" for Christmas. They had decorated every inch of the inn, with greenery and candles, red bows, and strings of dried apples. Grace and Margot had made moccasins for the little boys—Max and Kate's grandsons. Silas and Max had driven the buckboard to the train station, to pick them up two days before Christmas.

At last it was here, Christmas Day. The Inn at Thatcher Springs was full of family, joyful, happy, and turbulent with excited children. Tantalizing smells came from the kitchen, filling the place with what was to come. Millie had knocked herself out as usual, with the other women pitching in, baking breads, pies, cakes, and cookies. The family happily exchanged their simple gifts, mostly hand-made.

A new snow fell that day, adding to the foot already accumulated, which not only enhanced the beauty, but timing was perfect. "There's one more present," Merle said quietly and walked out back. When he returned, everyone gasped. "This here is for everbody." To the children's delight, Merle set a polished sled in the middle of the floor. It was made of wood with steel blades. "She'll take three or four at a time."

After a wonderful buffet dinner, as much as the men would rather be snoozing by the fire, they bundled up and took the kids out with the new sled. Eventually everyone went out to watch—everyone except Max and Kate. They cozied up in front of the crackling fire, just like old times. Well, not exactly like old times.

Each held a sleepy two-year-old on their lap. Kate stifled a giggle as she rocked little Eddie. "Can you believe it, Max? You're married to a grandma!" She laughed out loud then, startling the baby, nearly asleep. "Shhh. Grandma's sorry, sugar." But she continued to giggle into his soft hair.

Max handed her his coffee cup. "Here, ma'am, drink this stuff. It'll do ya a world a good."

"Oh Max. What a wonderful, blessed life we share." She snuggled Eddie closer and looked over at little Jonathon in Max's arms. "It's true, Max. Children are a gift from God." The peacefulness of the moment was shattered, when Jake burst in carrying Annie, who was full out bawling, blood coming from her nose. Max and Kate jumped to their feet, waking the little ones, who both began to cry too.

"Annie took a header," Jake explained, then kissed his little sister tenderly while still holding her. "It's okay, sweetheart," he said, his voice pitched up a notch. The whole bunch traipsed in behind them, tracking piles of snow and wetness, letting in cold air.

While everyone hung their coats and hurried to stand in front of the fire, Max and Kate calmed their daughter and helped the others out of their heavy jackets and boots. They were all talking at once, describing their various descents on Uncle Merle's sled, laughing cheerfully at the pileups, their cheeks like red apples.

Millie surprised everyone, kicking open the kitchen door and wheeling out a cart loaded with pies, cakes, cookies, and a pot of hot cocoa. "Time for dessert!" She smiled at Silas. "Could ya give me a hand, darlin? We're gonna set this up just like the table at our reunion." And then for his ears only, "Keep an eye on the wild Indians."

The family gathered around the fire singing carols, accompanied by Uncle Merle on the guitar and Hallie on the banjo. Millie directed Jake to the closet where the gutbucket was stored. "You go ahead and give it a try, honey. I'm plumb tuckered out." She had kicked off her shoes and curled up next to Silas, in front of the fire. Her eyes were closed. He hadn't seen her look quite so tired; it worried him a bit. *Hope she's okay, Lord. After all, we ain't spring chickens anymore.*

Millie rested like that for ten minutes or so, then suddenly sat up, wide awake. That familiar twinkle had returned to her eyes. "I have a wonderful idea! Let's all spend next Christmas at Seaside!" She clasped her hands together, bursting with thoughts for a family gathering. "That corner by the French doors would be perfect for a huge tree!" Her excitement mounted, until the other women began to lean forward, contributing more ideas. Josh and Joe looked at their wives with identical wonder as they jumped right in, adding to the conversation.

———

At last the inn was quiet. All the boys, from little Henry on up, had hauled their bedrolls to the bunkhouse, everyone else tucked in their beds sound asleep. All but Millie. She couldn't sleep. She was busy planning next Christmas in her mind. The winter moon cast a silvery light through the lace curtains, and for a moment, she thought she heard something. Quietly, she slipped over to the window. There was lamplight coming from the bunkhouse. Carefully, so as not to wake Silas, she raised the window.

Faintly at first, the music rose. It was Uncle Merle and a passel of boys, their singing filling the night air.

> Silent night, Holy night,
> All is calm, all is bright.
> Round yon virgin, mother and child
> Holy infant so tender and mild
> Sleep in Heavenly peace.
> Sleep in Heavenly peace.

Many years ago, Millie had looked out that same window often. Back then all she saw was darkness. Her life felt hopeless, bleak. She thought God had abandon her in those days. *But Lord, now I know you were always with me. You have blessed me beyond my wildest dreams and blessed this place called Thatcher Springs. I am so very thankful.*

She crawled back into bed, curling up against Silas, his strong arm pulling her close. Millie, with a smile on her lips, closed her eyes and fell asleep—soundly—in heavenly peace.

Printed in the United States
By Bookmasters